LIVING SPRINGS PUBLISHERS
PRESENTS:

STORIES THROUGH THE AGES
BABY BOOMER PLUS
2018

Compiled and edited by:
Henry E. Peavler, Dan Peavler, and Jacqueline Veryle Peavler

Introduction by Henry Peavler and Dan Peavler

Each story in this collection is a work created from the imagination or experience of the author. The views expressed in the stories do not necessarily reflect the views of Living Spring Publishers L.L.P.

Copyright 2018 by Living Springs Publishers LLP

ISBN: 978-0-9657113-6-4

Library of Congress Control Number: 2018909299

All right reserved including the right of reproduction in whole or in part in any form without written permission from the publisher

Living Springs Publishers
www.LivingSpringsPublishers.com

Cover design by Jacqueline Peavler

Cover Image:
Copyright: <a href='https://www.123rf.com/profile_sakkmesterke'>sakkmesterke / 123RF Stock Photo</a>

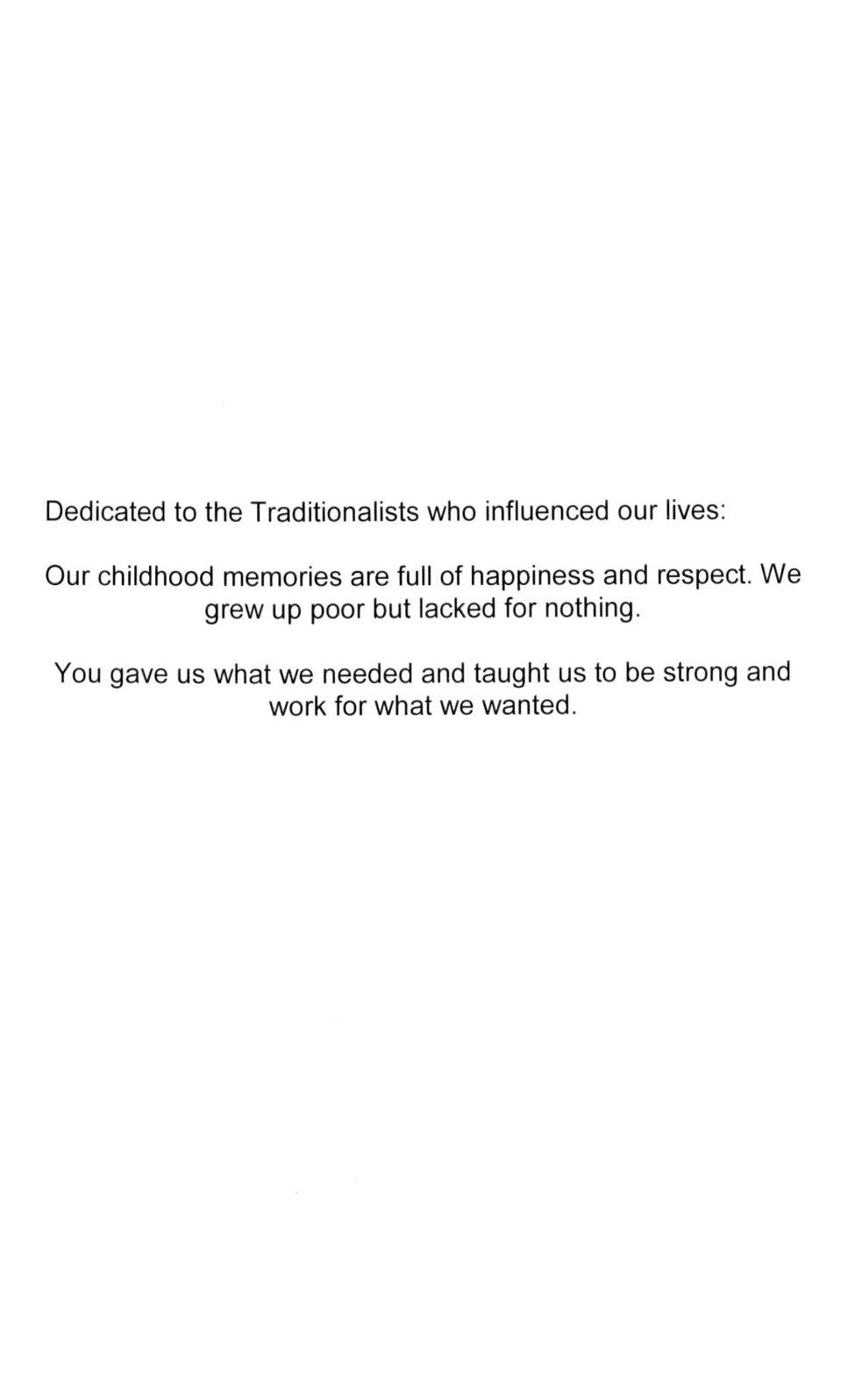

Dedicated to the Traditionalists who influenced our lives:

Our childhood memories are full of happiness and respect. We grew up poor but lacked for nothing.

You gave us what we needed and taught us to be strong and work for what we wanted.

Contents

SYNOPSES 1

INTRODUCTION 5

NEVER WORK FOR SOMEONE WHO'S NOT AS SMART AS YOU 7

DENNIS WINKLEBLACK 18

A WORTHY SPINE 19

PAM PARKER 34

SOFTENING SORROW 35

MARTHA WORCESTER 47

TRIAL BY WATER 48

LAURA BOLDEN-FOURNIER 54

GUARDIAN ANGELS CAME LATE 55

MARILYN V. DAVIDSON 67

LONGEST JOURNEY 68

RON L. DOWELL 81

HOCUS POCUS 82

JEAN ENDE 101

DUBS SECRET 102

RICK FORBESS 118

MONTEREY PAPA 119

DEBBIE FOWLER 134

WHISTLE IN THE FOG 135

GERALDINE HAWLEY 147

THE ONE THAT GOT AWAY 148

ERNESTO MARCOS 166

AN AMERICAN STORY 167

SUSAN MCLANE 178

SPYING ON THE GESTAPO 179

ROBERT L. NELIS 196

MISS MIMI'S CHARM SCHOOL 197

ANA THORNE 217

1200 RUPEES 218

NANCY ZUPANEC 234

LIVING SPRINGS PUBLISHERS 235

Synopses

First prize in this year's contest goes to Dennis Winkleblack. His story, **Never Work for Someone Who's Not as Smart as You**, is a hilarious chronicle of one young man's perception of himself and his life. Our hero looks at life through a filter that only he can perceive. We, the reader, can only sit back and laugh. A must read.

A Worthy Spine by Pam Parker is our second place finalist. In this irreverent look at the relationship between two sisters, Annie and Cora Matthews, who have lived together since the death of their husbands who happened to be brothers. Cora narrates this story from her death sentence diagnosis of breast cancer to the surprise ending. Funny, cheeky, bold you decide for yourself in this must read story full of well-defined characters and emotional relationships.

Our third place winner is Martha Worcester with her story, **Softening Sorrow**. Don't let the title fool you, this tale doesn't wallow in sorrow, it deals with the relationship between an elderly woman and her young next door neighbor in a magnificent and enlightened way. Jenny is a delightful little girl who meets Millie, who lives across the street. Both have issues that need each other to resolve. Wonderfully well-defined characters.

Trial by Water is a modern witch tale about a vigilante-type heroine who exacts justice for an elderly lady after she's exhausted all the other avenues. The author, Laura Boldin-Fournier, crafts an exquisite story steeped in the supernatural but believable at the same time. Although immoral, readers will applaud the heroine's method of resolving the problem.

Emotions run high in, ***Guardian Angels Came Late*** by Marilyn V. Davidson. In the 1980's, the horrors of domestic violence was still an often hidden social issue. In this harrowing first person account, a dedicated counselor and a mysterious bit of unexpected advice help an abused woman and her children escape from the nightmare that is their home.

Ron L. Dowell's ***Longest Journey*** is a delightful, lighthearted look at an elderly woman and her physical fitness obsessed son who does everything in his power to get her away from the television and out of her car. Funny and impertinent, this story is a must read just for the entertainment value but there is also an insight to be gleaned from the wisdom of those who have survived to a ripe old age. Don't miss Longest Journey.

Hocus Pocus, a wonderful story, full of insight and family relationships that are so well defined they could be any family. Written by Jean Ende, this is a chronicle of an immigrant Jewish family who bond together to care for a sick mother and watch over her two children. The youngest son decides to solve problems in his own way and the result is a surprisingly emotional scene that brings them together in a most unexpected manner.

Dub's Secret by Rick Forbess is a completely believable and well-written account of a legend that has become reality for two men who work together at a brick manufacturing plant. Ordinary men who live ordinary lives but become involved in an extraordinary adventure that had all the earmarks of a tragedy. The surprise ending is well crafted, as is the entire story, about men of faith who are confronted with an impossible situation.

In ***Monterey Papa***, Debbie Fowler, tells us about a journalist who makes a chance sighting of a familiar face in the crowd as she writes a story about the Monterey Pop Festivals from the 1960's. A fringe character from that era dies and a reminiscence of his life leads to unseen consequences for the journalist, Hildy, and her mother.

Geraldine Hawley's story, **Whistle in the Fog**, has Victorian overtones but is set in post-war London. Worthy of Poe or Dickens, a London Constable, new to the job, is confronted with an impossible situation. He saves the day, but accidentally, and then faces the prospect of explaining to his superiors something that could not have possibly happened. Or did it?

Ernesto Marcos gives us, **The One That Got Away**. This is a love story, in a way, but an unusual one and we aren't exactly certain what happens at the end. But that is part of the joy of this story and one man's remembrances of a time in his youth that he wants to recapture. A time when the man thought he had exactly what he wanted yet was unable to hold on to.

Susan McLane's ***An American Story*** takes us from immigrants in the hold of a 1740's sailing vessel bound for Pennsylvania to new parents in a South Carolina hospital in 1960. This chronicle of the intertwined lives of ordinary people is a fascinating study of how we become who we are. We are all products of those who came before, and that is never more apparent than in the lives of the characters in ***An American Story***.

Spying on the Gestapo, by Robert L. Nelis is one of those short stories that you can put down and when finished want to ask, 'is this true?' Juliette is recruited to spy on the Germans in occupied France. The challenges and dangers she experiences should be made into a movie. Wonderful story and well written.

Ana Thorne's entry, ***Miss Mimi's Charm School***, is a delightful story of a young girl, a bit out of her element, who handles the challenge with grace and wit. She and her father face the community prejudices when Inez attends a department store charm school. You'll enjoy Miss Mimi and all of the characters in this entertaining tale of young girls growing up in the 60's.

1200 Rupees by Nancy Zupanec does more than describe a camel trek into the Indian desert. The author takes us on a journey into a world of unknowns, physical and emotional, that she and her fellow travelers experience. Guides, camels, desert, and a glorious sunset are just the beginning of the adventure. Expect to learn more about human nature along with our heroine as she explores undiscovered places within herself.

Introduction

As stated in the old country lyrics "Yesterday is Dead and Gone" many people deem the true past lost forever. The authors of our second annual Stories Through the Ages Baby Boomer Plus Edition prove to disagree. Their nostalgic approach to writing allows some of us to reminisce and others to learn about times gone by. The many diverse and entertaining stories we received from authors across our great country and around the world allow us at Living Springs Publishers to publish a book of short stories that is truly entertaining.

With style and passion, the authors have given us knowledge from the heart, allowing us to experience the good along with the bad from the past. With genuine and profound flair, they have plied their story telling craft into memorable and engaging stories. They have shown us the dignity in dying and the beauty of living- that adversity can make everyday trials and tribulations seem unimportant.

It is our hope and goal for our contests to allow authors the freedom of expression and belief to write about whatever they wish to share. In a world that has culture constantly transforming, what is considered acceptable has changed and will change again in the future. Humankind can be analyzed through many different lenses. There is much power in writing when an author works without seeking approval or validation from others. We wish to allow authors an avenue in which they can convey about a time gone past, where there was a different moral fabric, in which they can write an account of the past, their understanding of the present or their vision of the future as seen through their eyes.

Thank you to all authors who submitted stories for the "Stories Through The Ages Plus 2018" contest. From science fiction to personal memoirs, throw in a bit of romance and tragedy, then add a comedy for the ages and you'll have a basic idea of the entertainment in this book. We could print an entire library from the wonderful stories that did not make the cut. But, then, that's the nature of a contest. We know how difficult it is to get published, that is a part of why we do this, but don't give up. Keep writing!

Never Work for Someone Who's Not As Smart As You
By Dennis Winkleblack

My advice? Never work for someone who's not as smart as you. You'll wish you hadn't, I guarantee it. Jealousy, I suppose, is what causes inferior people to act the way they do. They can't handle being wrong, having to say, "You were right, after all. Remind me not to question you again." Or, in Brian's case, admitting, "You should have my job, and I should have yours." Instead, they become all red-faced and make up facts as they go along.

For example, Brian said the project I hadn't started was due yesterday when I clearly remembered him saying "Wednesday", not "Monday" or "Tuesday" or whatever. Then he said I — **I** — have a problem with deadlines! I told him I haven't missed a deadline in my life, that he — **HE** — was the one who had problems with deadlines and facts, not to mention personal hygiene issues.

I mean, these pathetic human beings deserve to know why they're the unhappy, miserable creatures they are. Me? I'd sure want to know, if I were them, tell me straight out. But they're all, like, I'm Mr. or Ms. Big Cheese, and my poop doesn't stink. When you're a boss, you can get away with thinking like that, especially when you're trying to force a subordinate – a brilliant subordinate – to quit so they don't have to pay severance.

Like I said to Elena — she's my new neighbor, in the apartment above me — I told Elena while we were picking up our mail, "Never work for someone who's not as smart as you." She agreed and said I was a very lucky man to have figured this out before my 25th birthday. So, I asked her out for coffee. She was so honored that she hung her head and said, "Oh, wow! Holy crap!" Then she glanced up and rolled her eyes — I thought she was passing out — and said, "Sure, what the hell. How about Starbucks?"

Normally, I wouldn't go to Starbucks. Starbucks charges nearly five bucks for a cup of coffee that I know for a fact doesn't cost more than fifty cents. I don't understand. Why support such stupidity? But Elena had suggested Starbucks, so I said okay.

During our walk — it's on our block, so it was a short walk — she asked what kind of work I did. I told her accounting, which is the work I'd be doing if I were working at the moment. I did receive an accounting degree from Northeast College, even graduating with honors, though the college refused to print it in the graduation program because my Personal Income Tax professor, Horace Barnes, gave me a D simply because I was late to class and didn't finish the final exam. He knew I knew my debits and credits but wouldn't admit it, even when I went to his office to complain and he got all pissy and called campus security. Security was cool; the officer told me he'd heard Barnes screaming at me from his post at the entrance to the building. Said I shouldn't come back and wished me a good day. I wished him a good day, too. Nice guy.

Thing is, if it weren't for that D and the other Ds — and the F — I would've been honors, probably high honors. Sorry, but I can't recommend Northeast College. I don't care if they are ranked up there with Harvard. Still, I got my degree and then snagged a job right away. The job where Brian was my lame-o supervisor.

So, Elena and I took our coffees to our table. Elena ordered something with whipped cream running over the side of her cup. Me? Black coffee, size grande, whatever that means, which tasted like the other cup of Joe I'd had from Starbucks, with that burned-rubber flavor. Horrible. I'm positive they soak their beans in some kind of rubber extract so customers will think they're buying a highbrow concoction. Which they do because, as I said before, they're stupid!

I was also terribly disappointed with Elena. Since it was her idea to go to Starbucks, naturally I assumed she'd pay for my coffee. But that didn't happen. Luckily, I had my debit card. One thing led to another, and we got to talking about money, how I don't like to waste it. I proposed a hypothetical: say a gentleman was asked on a date by a girl to an expensive coffee shop — who should pay? At first, she acted like she didn't understand the scenario, but then she started to cry. Seriously! I asked if her shoes were too tight, or if her undergarments were pinching somewhere — I know mine certainly do if I pull them up too high. She didn't say yes, and she didn't say no, just hung her head like she'd done before. I couldn't think of what else to add, so I tried to finish my coffee — get my money's worth, at least. But, I'm sorry, rubber is rubber.

I'd barely returned from asking for my money back for the crappy coffee — which they gave me after I demanded to speak to the president of Starbucks — when Elena said she'd gotten a phone call saying her grandmother was dying. Or some relative — I'm pretty sure it was her grandmother. I offered to get her money back for her hardly drunk foamy-coffee disaster, but she shouted something that sounded like "you jerk" and said that if she never saw me again, it would be too soon. From my psychology class, I understand grief can have a strange effect on a person, cause them to feel inadequate. So, I grabbed at her hands — which were waving a lot — to express my sympathy.

When I finally latched onto her left one, she picked up her stupid coffee with the right one and accidently spilled it. Let me tell you, Starbucks coffee is nothing if not hot. Really hot. As in burn-your-crotch-to-pink-shreds hot.

This man — who'd been seated behind us — put his arm around my neck and pulled me away. He apparently thought Elena was attacking me and tried to save me. As I was setting him straight, Elena ran out the door, she was so ashamed of herself. Once she'd gone, the man was all kinds of mixed up, accusing me — **ME** — of being the perpetrator. I chalked it all up to the coffee Starbucks serves — I'm guessing the rubber-whatever they use causes mental instability. I thanked the man for his good intentions, re-tucked my shirt and walked toward the entrance, where another guy I hadn't seen before, but clearly a Starbucks employee considering his ugly uniform, stopped me. I assumed he would apologize for the disturbance, so I gave him my best smile because I didn't want him to think I was mad at Starbucks, though I had a good case, given their rip-off, way-too-hot coffee. Next thing I knew, this man, this Starbucks man, started saying stuff that made no sense at all, again confusing "that woman" and me so it was hard to tell what he assumed had happened. I assured him I'd make sure she never came back and told him he should see a doctor because drinking all that Starbucks coffee was definitely affecting his mind. You can be certain you've really gotten through to someone when they stare at you with their mouth open. I left before he could thank me.

I had my hand on the door handle of my apartment building when this dude handed me a flyer and said, "You're exactly the type we're looking for." The flyer had color pictures of two movie stars and the words, "Are you ready for a career in show business?" Well, heck, who isn't? Many nights I fall asleep dreaming of the day I'll be a star. I mean, I'm an experienced actor from back in high school. And, as my parents often remind me, Ridgeview High School is still talking about my ad libs in the production of Romeo and Juliet. The thing was, I thought it needed a few knock-knock jokes to add levity. And it worked — my skateboard buddies told me it was the best part of the whole shebang.

So, I've got show business creds, plus I'm tall or at least tallish, with most all of my hair, at least near the ears. As far as looks go, let's just say I can tell by people's reactions that I stand out. I'm sure you've seen how folks avert their eyes when they think someone's hot. They do that a lot when they see me coming. Not to mention my stout build, which alone marks me as someone so naturally endowed that he doesn't have to work out. No wonder people look at me with admiration. I'm not bragging, mind you, just giving the total picture.

Anyway, I asked this dude how much they paid, and he said, "It depends," which made sense — they can't know a person's full worth merely by looking at them on the street. Normally, I wouldn't agree to a job without more information, but having lost the accounting gig, I'd need to come up with rent money because my folks had only covered me for three months, plus the deposit and whatever, the usual this and that. So, I decided I'd at least listen to his pitch, run the numbers.

He wanted me to follow him up to the company's suite over Benson's, the eyeglass store. You'd think a big deal outfit from Hollywood would spend a lot on their offices, but this company didn't, which really sold me on their fiscal responsibility. "Fiscal" is a word I learned in accounting school. I use it as often as I can, like when the photography guy asked me where I worked and I answered, "I'm not working this particular fiscal year." It marks you as important, causes people to raise their eyebrows, when you use accounting words in everyday conversation. My experience, anyway.

I was looking through a Time magazine in their little waiting area, the issue with George Bush and Dick Cheney on the cover, when Mr. Miller — the "talent agent," he called himself — came from the back room with papers for me to sign. There was a camera on a tripod in the corner, so I asked him if he wanted to take pictures first so he could represent me better to studios and such. He said that wasn't how it worked, said I needed to pay him for the pictures in advance. Then he'd send them around and see what developed, but he had no doubt I'd be in six, seven figures annually very soon.

The price for the photos — $999 — wasn't the problem. It was that I didn't have that much dough on me. He suggested I put it on a credit card — he took a bunch of them — but I said I just had a debit card, though at the moment, in this fiscal year, I was running a low balance. I proposed, since it was guaranteed I'd make all kinds of money, that he front the $999 himself, that I'd reimburse him when I hit it big. I mean, wouldn't you do that? Got to spend money to make money, right? He must have been short himself because he said that was the most preposterous proposal he'd ever heard. I was sure the man was embarrassed to have to admit he was poor, so I didn't take it personally. He was so sorry to lose me as a client that he used a lot of sexually related words and kept saying "loser" over and over again. I told him not to beat himself up, that he'd find someone else even if they weren't quite like me. He was so sad, he slammed the door behind me. I'll definitely maybe check on him in a few days.

No sooner had I stepped out onto the sidewalk than I heard the shrillest siren and loudest school bell sound you can imagine shrieking across the street. The calamity was coming from the bank where I go. People were staring through the glass window, hands shielding their eyes from the sun's glare. Seemed to me a good time to wander over and check my account balance.

I crossed the street and pushed through the crowd, only to be slammed into by a couple of guys with paper bags over their heads coming out of the bank. Another paper bag — a heavy one — fell into my lap while I was on the ground. I opened it and saw all kinds of bills, but no change. Might have been a thousand dollars. Or more. So, I know you're thinking what I was thinking: it's about time!

I could hardly wait to get back to the Hollywood guy's place and tell him I'd forgiven him for his temporary insanity. The crowd parted when I stood and ran, but I hadn't gotten far when a hand — a big hand, the biggest hand I'd ever seen — latched onto my shoulder and stopped me in mid-stride. I was breathing heavily because, even for the shape I'm in, I must've run half a block. At least.

Turns out the big hand belonged to the bank security man who mistakenly thought I'd stolen the money. I told him nosireebob did I steal any money because thisheremoney was given to me. Told him I'd taken business law in college and knew my rights. I told him that if a party of the first part gives money to a party of the second part, the money belongs to said party of the second part. No ifs, ands or buts. He seemed good with it, but about that time, a couple of police cars pulled up.

I told the four officers plus police dog my story: laid off by Brian, Hollywood interview, no money, went to bank to get money, guy gave me bag of money, end of story. Party of first part, second part, yada, yada, yada. The police officers caught on immediately, laughing for the longest time at the mix-up. They called me a comedian, which I'd never been called before, but what a compliment! Maybe I should tell the Hollywood guy I'm also a comedian — I mean, why not? When the police guys insisted I come with them to tell the funny story to other police people at the precinct station, I said I would, no problem.

Soon, I was telling a roomful of police people plus the dog about Brian, Hollywood, no money, bank, bag of money, party of first part, second part, yada, yada, yada. Then, being a comedian and all, I added: "That's all, folks! I'll be here all week."

Laugh? You've never heard such laughter. One policeman laughed so hard, he had Coke coming out of his nose. The dog began to bark, which I guess is how they laugh. Bottom line, I was such a hit they insisted — **insisted** — I stay the night so I could tell the story over and over again, which I did. I'll share this tidbit with you for free: there's a lot to be said for having a toilet two feet away from your bed!

It's now the morning after, and I'm waiting for a Ms. Reynolds, whom they call a public defender. But as I explained to one of the detectives who was writing down my comedy routine word for word, as fun as it's been, I shouldn't stay much longer. That if they're unwilling to honor the law about the party of the first part, yada, yada, yada, then I'm going to have to look for a job. But he kept shaking his head, laughing now and then, finally asking me to sign my name saying the above was true. And, of course, I was glad to. I mean, it's my fiscal responsibility. Tell the truth, though, the way that detective was smiling at me, I thought for a minute that he'd offer me some kind of job right then and there. And, frankly, I would've been tempted — it was a nice place and all, what with the convenient bathroom setup. But I've learned my lesson: I'm through working for someone who's not as smart as I am.

END

Dennis Winkleblack

Dennis Winkleblack is a retired minister and lives in Connecticut. He is the author of three self-published books (Createspace) written under the pen name, Will Martin: Basically Good People; After Church Mysteries; and the novella, A Lucky Break. A short story, Twins, was included in the Zimbell House anthology, The Lost Door. He's currently working on a sequel to Basically Good People.

A Worthy Spine
By Pam Parker

Noah, better known in these parts as Dr. Solomon, reminds me of a basset hound. Always has. He was a slow-moving smart aleck back at Lincoln Elementary. But at this appointment, his droopy eyes are clouded with sadness. How old would he be? Fortyish? His pointer finger slides along the side of his mouth before he speaks.

I know what's coming before his words do. I've known for a while. My cancer is back. Different this time – I hadn't known the first time, didn't have a clue. Breast cancer can sneak up on you without a symptom, everybody thinks you'll feel a lump, you'll be tired, whatever, and for some folks, that's how it goes. Mine was full-blown when we found it, so odds were it would come back somewhere. Lately I've been tired, bone-tired, and that's not like me. I may be old but I've never been a lay around sort, and that's all I've been good for lately.

He pats my hand, covers my liver spots with his slender, straight fingers. "I'm sorry, Mrs. Matthews. The cancer's back and it's spread."

Ah, the death sentence, the final round.

Poor boy, trying so hard to maintain his professional demeanor. If I were someone else, he'd probably have more to say. Years back during cancer round one, I'd asked him to call me Cora, but he couldn't. To him I'll always be Mrs. Matthews, his old principal, or witch, take your pick. He wouldn't understand that I made my peace with dying a long time ago. After all, I've lived with Annie's dying for so many years. My baby sister, seventy-six years old, convinced she's been at death's canyon for the last umpteen years.

I thank him, head out to my old Impala, buckle in and sit there, glad it's not hot, not cold. I can keep the window rolled up and my skirt won't stick to the seat. A small relief. September days can be perfect in Kenosha. Leaning my head back, I close my eyes to see some nothing, but Annie appears behind my eyelids. I'm in no hurry to go home and tell her. Annie's not a hemorrhoid in my life these days, but she has been.. A serious pain in my ass at times.

About ten years back, the year spring hid in the snowdrifts longer than normal, that was the year Annie became certain she was dying. She had already lived through a lot of loss, so I couldn't quite understand her sudden slide into morbid-land. She wasn't whiny, just convinced she was on her way out. She knew that would be her last spring, assuming like the rest of us, that spring would arrive. And it did, tulips, daffodils, the whole colorful return, but Annie didn't lose her resolve. Every holiday after that would be her last. Every autumn's colorful extravaganza would be her last.

A chocolate ice cream cone with sprinkles?

Probably her last.

Melt in your mouth apple pie at the church fair?

Probably her last.

The certainty of her impending death arrived for no apparent reason and she's been "dying" ever since. No, not in the agonizing awful way that some people's bodies break down before the final heartbeat. Annie has been dying like the rest of us with reasonably good health, except we don't generally think about every breath being one closer to the casket lid. But since that dreary spring that took forever to kill our monochromatic winter, Annie's been stuck in doom and gloom.

I should be more sympathetic – don't think I don't know that. I'm her sister and I'm well aware of good reasons for some sadness. But there are so many days, so many cups of coffee shared when I want to shake her. Snap out of it. Come on. They're gone, we're not. Let's keep living until we're actually done. But I don't shake her or shout the things I want to. That counts as a bit of kindness, doesn't it?

Kind isn't the word that pops to mind when people think of me. I know that much. I imagine more than a few people in this town call me "bitch" behind my back. Some of that's because an elementary principal needs a bitchy nature dealing with parents and teachers. But Annie, she's always been sweet and good, simpering if you ask me. Born without a worthy spine.

We're old ladies now. No denying that. But Annie's old in the "giving in" kind of way, while I've been old in the "leave me alone" kind of way. I know what this generation would say, they'd say in the "f-you" way, but I can't quite let that word out of my mouth. Too old for that one.

A car door slams. An engine rumbles to life near me. I sit up a little more, check the rearview mirror and lean back again. Truth be told, if I could take a nap right here in the driver's seat, I would. But sleep isn't going to come, so I'll sit a couple more minutes. Me and my Impala and no whiny Annie.

Maybe it was a mistake to tell her to move in with me. She was so down I wondered if she'd think about the forbidden S word – you know, suicide. I really didn't think so because she clung to some faith and I wasn't sure how she'd work that out, but I was worried about her. And yes, I would feel guilty if she killed herself. And yes, I would miss her. A lot. Since it seems I'll be checking out first the big question is, what will happen to her?

The sun's gone behind a cloud and it's getting chilly in the Impala. I know, I know. I can't stay here forever. But I know what I'm doing. I'm riding the memory bus and nothing wrong with that. Might as well do it while I can without Annie fluttering around nearby, cooking this, washing that. A cup of tea, Cora? Did you take your Vitamin C this morning, Cora? Mind if I vacuum your room, Cora?

Christ.

Annie and I have lived what most folks would call normal lives. Even though she was the younger sister, she married first, Hal Matthews in the summer of '47. I married Fred Matthews in the summer of '49. Sisters married brothers – it happened more back then. We were neighbors on Stickney Avenue. Our men went downtown to work, Annie and I stayed in our homes. Take a dose of *I Love Lucy* and a dash of *Ozzie and Harriet* and you'll have the right idea. We added our kids to the baby boom. Our husbands kissed us good-by every morning, going off to earn money to buy our first televisions, our new refrigerators, our kids' piano lessons. They worked in that world we knew nothing of, with ledgers, secretaries, and board meetings.

You might think I was bored or jealous, but I was too damn busy. We had twin boys and that's when I learned for sure that I wasn't the best mother or housekeeper. It was a never-ending job to be Mommy Homemaker especially with my sister,

Polly Perfect up the road. Thought it would kill me but as you can see it didn't. Apparently, that will be cancer's job.

Annie and Hal had one son, Theo. I tried to talk her out of the name but in a surprising moment of stubbornness she wouldn't budge. "It sounds distinguished. Theo Matthews."

"That's not distinguished sounding. It sounds stupid, especially since you're not naming him Theodore and calling him Theo for short."

Annie harrumphed, quiet little Annie, the ever-following little sister. Harrumphing was definitely not in the job description for baby sister. Then she glared at me. At first, I was excited. See Annie is never one for a good old-fashioned debate or argument. That girl sniffs conflict and retreats, either inside herself or from the room. She sidesteps anything prickly the way kids skip over sidewalk cracks.

I thought maybe she would let me have it, but no.

She sat there in her gingham, patting her curls, then wedging a knife through a cinnamon-scented coffee cake. "If it's a boy, his name will be Theo and you have nothing to say about it."

A little anger? A rising pitch? Anything? No. That was it. She put me in my place and ended the discussion. No fun at all.

So Theo got stuck with a ridiculous name, poor kid. Was his downfall I think, but I'd never say that to Annie. I can be blunt, but even I know that's an "I told you so" that can never be spoken. I'm not cold-hearted. My Fred knew that. I still miss him.

We're widows, me and Annie. My Fred died too young – heart attack took him at thirty-nine. I went back to school, became a teacher and then a principal, worked my fanny off outside the house, and couldn't care less about the mess in our home. My boys grew up a little rougher around the edges than I wish they had, but they did all right. Come to think of it, being on their own so much might have served them better than the clingy way Annie raised Theo, not that I'm judging. As for my twins, Tom and Mike, I understand it's not an easy thing for boys to navigate those awful teen years without a father and I wasn't able to play the dutiful mother role as much as I should have. Putting money in the bank was necessary and it meant spending my energy on other people's kids. That's what had to be done. The twins survived, went to college and grad school, avoiding the heave-ho to Vietnam and that was fine with me.

They both moved to Chicago – good wives, nice kids. They've built themselves good lives. I see them now and again. I always thought it was better for Annie that they weren't around so often, might remind her too much of Theo.

That was a hell of a time. Didn't see it coming. Just a couple years from my retirement Annie and Hal invited me to join them on a summer trip to the Grand Canyon. Why not, I thought. I hadn't been anywhere. Two weeks before we were supposed to go, we got word that Theo had died out in California. Drug overdose. I wondered about AIDS. Pretty sure Theo was gay and that's when AIDS was all over San Francisco, but we never talked about it. Annie wouldn't have been able to face that. She's got that Catholic guilt thing deep in her marrow. I bled it out a long time ago.

Theo had flunked out his first semester at UWM and enlisted. Vietnam and a cursed name did that boy in, you ask me. He got back from the jungles with his parts intact, but he'd found drugs over there. He took off to San Francisco and maybe he had some good times. I do hope that. Hope it wasn't all torture and misery and drowning his sorrow in pills or pipes, or whatever it is they do.

Never did get to the Grand Canyon.

Don't want to spend my memory train ride on anymore of those bitter days. The thought of them lingers like the taste after choking down bad medicine. I worried we'd lose Annie then, but we didn't. It was Hal who checked out – within nine months of Theo's funeral, we were planting Hal beside him. Another bad heart attack. I warned my boys – you've got the heart attack gene, so take care of yourselves. Then I got scared about Annie, and I guess, to be honest, about me too. I mean people dying too close together like that can shake anybody up. I decided to quit working and enjoy myself.

I retired a year sooner than planned and ordered Annie to move in with me. It didn't take much ordering. She couldn't stand being in her house and I didn't have to worry about cleaning mine anymore. It wasn't the best or the worst arrangement. It was what it was, that's what folks say now. Ridiculous expression if you ask me. It was one of those "no choice" deals life hands us every now and again. Annie was so grateful it hurt. I thought if I heard, "thank you, Cora," one more time I would have slapped her. But she paid me back when she hauled me to chemo and put up with me. I was pissed off at how sick I got. Probably was a real bitch. Seemed a waste of time.

Won't go through that again. Definitely not.

And that's the last thought I need to fire up the car and drive back home.

Soon as I open the door, I smell something on the stove, celery, onions and chicken. She's making chicken soup again. Keeps the cold germs away she says.

"Any news, Cora?"

"Nope, everything's fine." I hook my purse on the chair and sit at the table with my back to her. Not being rude, just in my usual spot. Annie brings me over a bowl of chicken soup and a spoon. I realize I'm hungry and glad for the soup. "Thanks." Besides, I have to think about how to tell her, my delicate crystal sister. I am her last connection to a time in her life that was happy. Can she stand alone? Annie? Hard to believe it's possible. One thing I know is I don't want to die thinking I'd hurried up my sister's demise.

I shake some salt over my bowl and hear Annie's sigh at the stove. She always says I use too much. Going to be dumping in the shaker soon - won't make any difference. The faucet's on at the sink and I wonder if she's looking out the window. If she sees the last board from the tree house that just won't fall off the old maple? The tree house makes me think of the twins. Can my boys step up and watch out for their Aunt Annie? Not likely. Their lives are hectic, kids finishing high school, looking at colleges. How are they going to fit in a depressed aunt when their mother kicks that infamous bucket?

***

October has come and gone. It was a glorious gold one. The sugar maples never showed off as much before. I almost slipped and said to Annie that I hoped to go out like that, in a blaze of orange glory. Nope, haven't told her yet. I know, I know I have to, but I don't want to. And since the Grim Reaper's got my number, I don't have to do anything I don't want to. Yes, I've adopted a three-year old's attitude. Too bad.

Did I tell you Noah said the cancer's in my bones?

My ribs are killing me. Maybe literally. Ha.

Tom calls, invites me and Annie down for Christmas. "Don't think we'll be down this year," I say from the rocker with the red corduroy tie-back cushion. My most comfortable spot these days.

Annie looks up from her knitting, question marks forming in her eyes.

I babble something about my arthritis flaring and Tom starts making noises about coming up to us.

"No, no, don't you worry. We're just fine."

Annie walks over and mouths. "Can I talk to him?"

I shake my head.

She hollers out, "I'll call you later, Tommy."

"What's going on, Mom?"

"Nothing, we're fine. But I have to go now." I hang up.

"Cora, what is going on? We always go there for Christmas," Annie says.

29

"I'm tired. And my back is really sore – I don't want to do that car trip. All that Chicago traffic, the potholes on the roads…"

Annie sets her knitting down. Fluffs the rooster pillow on the couch.

That pillow's going in the trash this afternoon. Never liked that damn rooster.

She presses her hands on her knees. "I know something's going on. You haven't been yourself since you got back from your appointment with Dr. Solomon last month."

Crap. Am I going to have to tell her?

"Do you think I'm stupid?" She sounds, what is it? Hurt? Annoyed?

"No. I don't think you're stupid." A whiny pain-in-my-ass sometimes, but not stupid.

"Then tell me the truth. What is going on with you?"

Why do I have to face this moment? I shut my eyes. Why couldn't I have just died in my sleep last night?

"Look at me, please."

I don't open my eyes or move.

"Come on. Don't lie to me. What did Dr. Solomon say?"

"All right, all right." I sit back, pressing my shoulder blades into the cushion. "It's back. The cancer's back."

Sadness registers in her fading-blue eyes. "When does treatment start?"

"I'm not doing treatment."

"But..."

"No buts. I already told Noah. He said I might have four good months or more before the pain gets really bad. Then I told him to medicate the hell out of me so I'm out of it."

She stands up and opens her mouth, turns and looks out the bay window. "You're in pain now though, aren't you?"

"Yes." No sense lying about that. "It's going to be all right, Annie."

She sits back down on the couch, sits up straight like her vertebrae have fused together in a straight line. Like her spine may never bend again. She drops her hands in her lap. Her eyes fill with tears.

I brace myself for the coming waterworks, the pity party, the "what will happen to me" chorus.

"For once, for once in your damn life will you admit it's not going to be all right? You are going to... to die.... aren't you?" Using her napkin, she wipes her eyes with purpose, seems mad at her own tears.

I laugh. I know, I can be cruel, but come on. "Of course I'm dying. So are you -- one of these days you'll go, too."

"Everything doesn't have to be on a laugh track either. It's okay to be sad. This is a time when it's really okay to be sad."

"I don't intend to go out sad."

She stands up. "Let's have a cup of tea."

I follow her into the kitchen. Tea is Annie's answer to everything.

I sit at the kitchen table, not loving the view of naked forsythia branches scratching the window over the sink.

Annie sets our mother's china cups down with Earl Grey bags in them, then waits near the stove. The kettle whistles. She fills our cups and sits down, bobs her teabag in the hot water. "Well, just know that I will take care of you, whatever you need, whenever you need it, I'm here."

A sense of relief I hadn't known I needed settles on my chest. The oak tabletop reflects a sunbeam from the window. Guess I'll have to tell the boys the truth soon. But Annie? What will happen to her? I don't want to talk about that yet.

"And don't think I don't know you, Cora. I know you better than you know yourself. You can stop worrying about me. I'll be fine. If there's one thing you've taught me these last couple years, it's that living needs to be my focus while I'm walking around."

My head lifts, my heart lifts. She stands, gray, short and shriveling, but not simpering. In fact, Annie stands strong.

Didn't expect to live to see that.

Pam Parker

Pam Parker, a New England native who lives in greater Milwaukee, WI, has worked in public relations and teaching, but now devotes her time to writing and traveling. She is an MFA candidate at Sierra Nevada College. Her stories have appeared in print and online journals, including THE POTOMAC REVIEW, THE MACGUFFIN, GREY SPARROW PRESS and more. Her essays have appeared in THE WASHINGTON POST (and then by syndicate in many more papers in the U.S., Canada & New Zealand), QUEEN MOBS TEAHOUSE, in two anthologies FAMILY STORIES FROM THE ATTIC and DONE DARKNESS. A regular contributor to her local public radio station - WUWM Lake Effect, her audio-essay, "The End of Pinktober," received a 1st place large market audio-essay award from the WI Broadcasting Assoc. Additional work has been recognized by the WI Academy of Arts, Sciences & Letters and the WI Writers Assoc. Links to some of her writing and speaking can be found at pamwrites.net.

SOFTENING SORROW
BY MARTHA WORCESTER

Jenny's mother said the night before, "No school tomorrow, you can sleep late." The sun's bright light shining on Jenny's bed begged her to get up. It was 10 0'clock, the first Monday after school ended for the summer. She dressed quickly, found her mother standing at the sink in the kitchen, and announced. "I'm going outside, Mama."

"Not till you eat something, Honey." Her mother set a box of cheerios on the table and a small pitcher of milk. Jenny pushed a chair up to the table and climbed onto it. Her legs dangled under the chair. She was shorter than most kids in her class. Impatient to be outside, she set her legs in motion, swinging them back and forth while she spooned cheerios into her mouth. She eyed her mother's back to be sure she wasn't looking before putting her lips to the bowl's rim to drink the last of bit of milk and slid off the chair.

Jenny's mother turned from the sink, collected the bowl and pitcher and rumpled her daughter's red curly hair. "Okay you can go out now. Remember, don't go across the street without asking me."

Jenny skipped to the front door and let the screen slam behind her. She sat on the stoop trying to decide what to do next. The dusty pot-holed street in front of the house was empty of cars, as usual. Only a few passed by each day. Pineville, population 3500, was tucked in among the mountains of Northern California. Seasons there were sharply divided into three months each. Winters held deep snows. Spring thaws arrived on schedule in late March with a profusion of wildflowers. Summers, though hot and dry, were made bearable by mountain breezes. Falls were cool and colorful with leafy deciduous trees blended well among tall pines and long-needled ponderosas. Jenny and her parents had moved to Pineville at the start of the last school year.

Jenny liked the feel of the warm sun. She stuck her bottom lip out and creased her forehead wishing her classmates were nearby. Most lived too far away for Jenny to go there alone. She had no big brothers or sisters to accompany her. She studied the big gray two-story house across the street and tried to imagine what the rooms were like inside. The lawn was overgrown and uneven with dandelions peeking out here and there. The low fence surrounding the lawn was in disrepair. Leaning fence posts barely supported the large squared wire fencing and the boards framing the top sagged. She remembered her mother saying, "Now don't you go bothering that old woman, and don't go across the street without asking me first."

***

The old woman was mowing her lawn at the side of the house, and came around to mow the lawn in front. Her long white hair streamed down her back. The breeze caught a few strands and blew them crosswise tickling her face. She had oiled the rusty mower blades and connecting points between the wheels and axles the evening before. She was pleased the mower rolled smoothly over the bumpy lawn, leaving a path through the tall grass.

She stopped to straighten her aching back. With one hand on the mower handle to steady her balance, she brushed strands of hair and beads of sweat from her face. She looked at her gray weather-beaten house with the big screened-in porch. None of the original paint remained. The colorless gray was now uniform. Millie argued with herself for the hundredth time, "You should paint it to protect those old boards; but I like the look of it the way it is. The roof needs to be replaced; but it doesn't leak and it will likely last at least as long as I do."

Glad she had hung onto the house, Millie had returned ten years ago to take up residence. She inherited the house from her parents after their death in an auto accident on her 25th birthday. At the time Millie was working in Chicago for a law firm as a paralegal. Despite all the Pineville house's troublesome renters and fights with the property manager, she was never able to bring herself to sell it.

"Can I really be eighty years old?" Millie wondered how she managed to live through three miscarriages, a failed marriage, and that short liaison with a man she hardly knew. The liaison had resulted in her only daughter. Much about the man had faded from her memory, yet she clearly recalled his displeased look when she told him she was pregnant. He didn't say a word, touched her hair, turned away and went out the door. He never contacted her again. She became unsure if he'd even given her his right name. She had not asked where he lived or worked and found she had no interest in trying to contact him again. Her paralegal work had taught her the futility and cost of tracking down fathers of children. She found the legal work rewarding and it gave her the security needed for raising her child. Since then she had not been willing to trust a man enough to love her daughter the way she did.

Half done with mowing the front yard, Millie paused to gather her strength. Her gaze shifted to the child sitting on the stoop across the street. The child had sold her California poppies a few days back. "A penny a piece, she'd said." Millie bought them all. She remembered the freckles sprinkled across the small child's checks and nose and thought she must be about five or six years old.

Millie felt tears on her cheeks and a deep ache rising in her chest. She took a deep breath and stood awhile, letting the tears come. Memories flooded in of her daughter Melanie. Tears falling were not a new experience for Millie. She wondered what had brought them on just now. She looked again at the child on the stoop. She didn't look anything like the child she'd lost. She smiled through the tears. She knew. It was the child's posture. Leaning forward with elbows resting on her knees, palms of hands holding up her chin. It was a pose Melanie had often assumed.

Memories of the day Melanie died washed over Millie. She firmed her balance, gripping the lawn mower handle with one hand, while raising her other arm to wipe tears from her face and chin. Though thoughts of Melanie ebbed and flowed, now the memory of the day her seven-year-old daughter died was crystal clear. Millie walked slowly up the stairs, through the screened in porch, front room, and dining room, steadying her gait on chairs strategically placed to prevent a fall, a fear that haunted her.

In the kitchen, she leaned against the counter and took in a big breath before tugging hard on the fridge door. The door, usually stuck, opened without a whimper throwing her a bit off balance. She was prepared for its unpredictability and had braced herself against the counter and widened her stance. The ice build-up around its freezer compartment required another forceful tug.

Standing over the sink, she turned the tap and watched the water filter down between the cubes till the glass was full. She felt the cold water slide down her throat. The ache in her chest subsided. The memory of that long-ago day was as clear to her as the cool water's refreshment was to her dry mouth. She walked with the glass into the dining room, and sat down on one of the matching chairs at the large oval table. The table and chairs, together with hutch on one side and brimming bookcases on the other, left barely enough space to walk through the room.

An old frayed-at-the-edges lace cloth covered the table's surface and hung halfway to the carpet below. Plates, cups, and saucers, arranged in neat stacks, covered half the table. The hutch stood waiting for the dishes to find their place beside collections of old teacups, platters, and mementos already in residence behind its glass doors.

Millie, engulfed in her memories, glanced at the dishes on the table without seeing. She was in her second floor Chicago apartment, with the window wide open, collecting a bit of breeze on a hot summer day. She heard the screech of tires, the car door slam, a loud scream. Then, "Oh No!" She scanned the room to see where Melanie was. Her hand came to her throat, just as it had that day long ago. She leaned out the window, and caught sight of the pink tennis shoe of the small figure lying on the ground. She stumbled down the stairs and ran into the middle of the street and knelt beside a sobbing girl. The girl covered her face with her hands and leaned on Millie's shoulder, moaning, "Oh, God tell me she's not dead! Please, tell me she's not dead."

Millie felt afresh, the nausea rising in her stomach as she bent to place Melanie's head in her lap. The sobbing girl rose and ran away. An ugly gash stood out on Melanie's forehead, and Millie felt the blood from the wound seep into her skirt as her daughter gave one last gasp, and was still. Memory of the rest of that day she could never recover. Nothing beyond the moment when her child lay heavy and lifeless in her lap.

Her co-workers filled her in on all the details. The teenage driver had called the ambulance and returned to await its arrival. The girl stood silent with tears streaming down her face as the medics lifted the body from Millie's lap and carried it to the ambulance. No siren.

Millie's tears stopped. The deep ache in her chest diminished and she sat down to rest. Her eyes drifted to the large volumes on the bottom shelf of the bookcase. The letters on their two-inch spines were still legible despite their age. *The Wonderful Wizard of Oz, The Emerald City, The Tin Woodsman, The Cowardly Lion...* a series of seven altogether. Their bright colors had faded over time and they begged to be dusted. She bought them more than 50 years ago, five days before the accident.

A vision of her daughter with the exact same pose as the little girl across the street and a plea of "There's nothing to do, Mommy," had prompted Millie to take her daughter shopping. Melanie discovered the Oz books on a shelf in the store, arranged at just the right height to tempt a young child. They cost more than Millie wanted to spend. She couldn't resist the "Please, Mommy, please," recited over and over as she tried to pull her away from the book shelf. Millie talked the supervisor into a payment plan which allowed her to take the books home that day. They planned to start reading them together after supper, the day of the accident.

She sighed and bent to pick up one of the volumes. Her back reminded her of the reason so much dust had collected. Taking in a deep breath, she emptied the glass and rose. "Well the lawn has to be mowed," she said aloud. She opened the screen door and looked across the street. The stoop was empty. She looked down toward her unfinished mowing and noticed the child leaning on the fence. She looked up at Millie, "Can I help you mow the lawn?"

Millie smiled slowly, opened the gate and held out her hand. The child drew back. Millie dropped her hand, and opened the gate wider.

"Come on in the yard, child." Millie stepped aside to let her pass. "What's your name?"

"I'm Jenny," was the almost inaudible answer.

"I know you haven't lived here long. I wondered what your name might be. Gracious, it's hot out here. It's much cooler in the house. Come inside, I'd like to show you something."

Jenny followed, glancing back across the street as Millie opened the screen door.

"It's okay, Jenny, I'll let your mother know I invited you in."

Jenny smiled and trailed Millie up the steps to the screened-in porch, through the front door with the scratchy oval glass in the center, across the spacious living room and into the cramped dining room. The dusty staleness made Jenny's nose crinkle. Her eyes struggled to adjust to the dim light inside. She looked up at crowded clusters of small ceramic figures on narrow corner shelves. Millie noticed and took one down, dusted it with her sleeve, and handed it to Jenny. Jenny sneezed as she reached for it. She slid her hands over the smooth ceramic glaze of the figurine. She looked closely at the ceramic doll and the hat on its head.

"It's a nurse. It's so pretty. When I grow up I'm going to be a nurse," she announced, handing it back to Millie.

Millie returned the doll to its place, and pointed to the big bookcase. "Jenny, see the books on the bottom shelf there. Can you dust them off for me? My old back won't let me lean over that far."

She handed Jenny a tattered cloth. While Jenny dusted, Millie watched the dust particles become airborne and reflect the sun streaming through the side window. Jenny read the names of the titles: "*The Tin Woodsman, The Cooowaarrdleee Lion.*" She sounded out each one as she finished dusting it.

"How old are you Jenny?"

"I'm eight. I'll be in third grade next year! Do the books have pictures?"

"Yes, lots of pictures."

Jenny tugged on *The Wonderful Wizard of Oz*, pulled it off the shelf and it fell over on its side. She drew the bulky volume onto her cross-legs and let it open into the lap of her dress. She fingered the gritty stiff pages. She paused at bright colored sketches of munchkins, monkeys, the tin woodman. "The paper looks like newspaper, but it's thick and the letters are bigger," she said.

"You can borrow the book. When you finish, bring it back and you can borrow the next one."

Getting to her feet, Jenny managed to pick up the *Wonderful Wizard of* Oz. She brought it to her chest, and walked slowly across the room. Millie held doors open for her as she passed through the house and stood watching as Jenny first stopped and looked both ways before crossing the street. Jenny's mother was standing outside her front door and waved at Millie as Jenny disappeared inside.

***

Thus, began the summer, with Millie delighting in watching Jenny come skipping across the street. Jenny's presence fostered in Millie an ebb and flow of sorrows. The sorrow began to soften. Memories of good times she had with her daughter came bubbling up when Jenny laughed. A pattern of warmer memories of her daughter became tightly woven together with the day of the accident.

Millie was startled the first time she heard her own laughter, dormant over so many years. She had come here to be alone. The old house had given her the sense of peace she craved and eased the pain of dreams lost. Yet with Jenny, there came a fresh measure of contentment. She heard her own laughter mingled with the child's. She treasured the feel of Jenny's small body leaning against hers. Millie brought out other books lingering on the dusty shelves of the bookcase. They were books Millie read with Melanie before the Oz books were purchased. She enjoyed Jenny's pleasure as they took turns reading aloud to one another.

Toward summer's end, Millie was sitting on her front porch swing and looked up to see Jenny slowly walking across the street hugging the last of the big volumes to her chest. A car approached, saw Jenny, and braked. Millie, hand at her throat, closed her eyes. Hearing nothing, her eyes opened. The car had stopped in time. Jenny hadn't even looked up.

Still shaken, she noticed Jenny's usual smile was gone. Jenny frowned as she climbed the porch steps with the big book. Millie held the door open. Jenny walked into the dining room. Millie followed behind. Kneeling on the floor, Jenny wedged the big book back onto its place on the shelf and let her fingers run across the backs of all of the thick volumes.

"I read them all, Miss Millie." Her usual smile returned as she closed her hand around the fingers of the hand Millie offered. "When I get old, I will have a big gray house. I'll let my hair grow long and find a lawn mower to push, just like yours."

Millie felt her throat tighten. No words came. What escaped was something between a laugh and a sob. Her hand tightened around Melanie's. They walked out to the porch and settled into the gentle rock of the swing.

Martha Worcester

Martha Worcester began writing at age 75. She enjoys writing most about the lives of older adults. Stories she writes start with a core of truth from her own life experiences. They grow as she writes to become more like creative non-fiction. They evolve from memories of older adults as a child, her past nursing career, and her current work at Senior Centers where she facilitates a variety of groups and works with individuals to assist them in meeting challenges life brings beyond age 65. She calls her work with elders *Keys to Aging: Late Life Design.* She is especially thankful for the editing and encouragement she receives from writing workshop teachers and her monthly writing group.

"Writing gives me a voice to describe for others the many paths of life taken in old age. It opens wide the doors to my own memories and imagination. So many authors whom I've never met have added dimensions to my life I would never have known except through reading their work. I publish to give back to the writing and reading world what so many have given and continue to give to me."

Trial by Water
By Laura Boldin-Fournier

Judging from the stained sofa and dusty furniture, no one had cleaned Mrs. Reilly's home since Eisenhower was president. The old lady invited me to sit down. "I wasn't expecting a young woman," she said.

It wasn't the first time my appearance had surprised someone.

Mrs. Reilly gently lowered herself into a rocking chair. Her frizzy white hair stuck out in forty-two different directions. Most likely, it'd been a long time since she'd changed clothes and combed her hair. She wrung her hands. "It's hard to talk about."

"Some things are," I sniffed the musty air. A mangy cat stuck its head out from under the couch. I wondered if the new suit I'd worn would smell like cat urine when I left. I didn't have time to change before my next appointment, another meeting with a senior citizen. Disgruntled baby boomers provided me with most of my business.

Mrs. Reilly stood. "You should look at the basement first."

"Why?" It seemed like an odd request. Maybe the woman was senile.

"That's where it happened."

"What?"

"I'll tell you . . . after you see the basement." She walked across the room, opened a door and pointed. "Down there."

I shrugged. Oh, well. It wouldn't hurt to humor her. Holding onto a rail, I descended.

She stood at the top of the staircase, watching me. "Be careful. The last three steps are under water."

Covered with mold, the damp cement walls reeked of decay. Halfway down the slimy staircase, I sneezed.

"Bless you," Mrs. Reilly called.

Murky water swirled over the floor. I'd seen enough. I headed back upstairs. "I'm not a plumber," I said. "Are you sure you called the right person?"

She nodded. "I think so." When she returned to her chair, the cat leaped onto her lap and curled up. She stroked its back. Looking at Mrs. Reilly's long black dress and her cat brought to mind the image of a witch. "When I called Mr. Karma's office, I didn't expect him to send a young woman."

Now that she'd mentioned it a second time, I'd have to explain. "I'm Mr. Karma's assistant." That was a lie, but the less she knew about me, the better. "All I do is gather information and report to the boss. Nothing more."

"My husband and I moved here five years ago. As soon as it rained, the basement flooded. We lost the oil burner and everything stored there. An engineer said that our builder laid the foundation over an underground stream. The builder refused to help us, so we sued him."

"And then?"

"Nothing came of it. He closed his business and declared bankruptcy, but somehow he manages to live in a mansion."

"Life isn't always fair."

"Neither is death," she said.

"I can't disagree with that."

She took a deep breath and then blurted, "My husband died because of that water."

"He drowned?"

"No." She shook her head. "A snake came in with the water. It startled Harry. He slipped and broke his neck."

"I'm sorry."

She dabbed her eyes with a tissue. "Harry was my whole life."

"Do you have any children?"

"We wanted to, but we never did." She closed her eyes for a moment, then continued. "I dream of Harry all the time. I can't forget what happened. I need justice."

"I understand."

She withdrew a crumpled envelope from her pocket and passed it to me. "This is all I can afford."

I glanced at the cash inside. "You could use this money to repair your home."

"I won't live here much longer."

"You're moving?"

"I'm dying," she said. "I only have a few more months. I can't leave the world knowing that rich builder's living the good life in his mansion." She handed me a card with a name and address on it. "Will your boss take care of this?"

"He'll handle it."

Her eyebrows drew together. She bit her lip, as if ashamed of her decision. "Nobody should have to do this."

I stuck the business card in my pocket. "Sometimes there's no other choice."

I shadowed the builder for days. She was right. He was wealthy, and he did live in a mansion. Three acres of exquisitely landscaped grounds extended behind his home. Every afternoon, I lurked in the shade of the woods. Hiding in the shadows. Watching. Waiting.

One afternoon, he emerged wearing sunglasses and a headset. His sandals flapped against the cement as he walked toward the pool. After turning a lounge chair to face the sun, he reclined.

He didn't move as I approached. Maybe he'd fallen asleep. I leaned over and pulled off his sunglasses and earphones.

He blinked, startled. "Who the hell are you?"

"Mrs. Reilly lost her husband because of you."

"Who?"

This creep didn't even remember her.

"I don't know what you think you're—"

"Call me Karma."

"Crazy's more like it." He glared. "Get off my property before I throw you off."

"Not yet."

He made a fist and stood.

I kicked the back of his knee. He buckled over and went down, slamming his head on the concrete. I rolled him into the swimming pool. He sank to the bottom and stayed there.

Long ago in Salem, they conducted witch trials by immersing women in water. If a woman floated, she was judged guilty. Innocent people drowned before they were pulled out. Life isn't always fair. Neither is death. But once in a while, karma balances the scales.

THE END

Laura Bolden-Fournier

Laura Boldin-Fournier is a former teacher and librarian who writes for all ages. She lives in Florida, but would consider moving to a place where pizza and chocolate don't have calories. Because she's an animal-lover, her favorite spot to write is near a window where she sees lizards, birds and squirrels in the field behind her home. Laura's a member of the Society of Children's Book Writers and Illustrators and the Mystery Writers of America. She's a contributor to CHICKEN SOUP FOR THE SOUL books and magazines. One of her short stories won a contest sponsored by wordsandbrushes.com. Her humorous children's book, AN ORANGUTAN'S NIGHT BEFORE CHRISTMAS was published by the Pelican Publishing Company and is available on Amazon. Follow Laura on twitter and learn more about her at lauraboldin.com.

Guardian Angels Came Late
By Marilyn V. Davidson

Mistakes taught me how to make better decisions in my life—with a little help from guardian angels. My parents did a good job of teaching me how to make good decisions and for that I give them credit. Loneliness after high school, then love and confusing emotions interfered with what I thought I knew about decision-making. Various methods of decision-making are an often neglected or ignored life skill on our journey to adulthood and it is at this time that they are the most needed.

I know. It happened to me. After graduation, I was off to college, but a family crisis robbed the savings for my future education. Scholarships, grants and student loans were not common back then. Work was the next best thing. I got a full-time job and saved up for my first semester of college classes. When school started I continued to work.

One day, I collapsed in a college hallway. My mom took me to the doctor. He told said that I was suffering from exhaustion and needed to choose college or work, but I was not able to do both at the same time. The strain was more than I could handle. I reluctantly chose work. I thought if I saved my earnings I could then go to college.

Six months later, my sister introduced me to her boyfriend's brother. After dating him for six months, he joined the armed services and proposed marriage. I accepted, but broke the engagement six months later after giving it considerable thought. He came back and proposed again. He convinced me and we married a year later. My parents and older brother didn't approve, but I didn't heed their advice.

The decision to accept his proposal was a huge mistake. After we married and moved a thousand plus miles from my family, to where he was stationed, he became abusive. He took great pleasure in scaring me in any way he could think of, with guns and rattlesnakes. He was both mentally and physically abusive, especially while I was pregnant.

I was not raised in an abusive family. I was a devout Christian and took my marriage vows seriously. I finally decided to leave, but learned that I was pregnant. I didn't want my kids to grow up in a broken home. Therefore, I tried to make the best of it. Each time he abused me; he apologized afterward and promised that he would never do it again. I believed him the first several times he made that promise, but I became worn down and lost another a little piece of my personal resolve each time I suffered his abuse.

The physical abuse was varied. He flung me against walls, against sliding doors and into appliances. He said he *accidentally* fired a shot at me from a hair-triggered gun and almost hit me. He tried to rape me after we came home from a Christmas party. He was angry because I danced once with his friend, but he failed to complete the rape because he passed out from the alcohol he consumed at the party.

Once, I tried to call the police and he ripped the phone out of the wall. We went hunting when I was pregnant. While I waited in the car and read a book, he shot and killed a rattler. He crept up behind me and held the snake's head up by the side of my head. He called my name; I turned, and saw it. He laughed with glee while I screamed, and was completely terrified. I wore long sleeves all the time to cover the bruises, but I protected my children at all costs. Yet, the violence took place in our home and they were scared and hid under their beds when it occurred. I tried hard to give them a semblance of normalcy. I engaged them in activities that would keep them happy and physically active. I took the children to church and taught Sunday school regularly. My husband refused to go to church with us. I knew the Scripture said, "God helps those who help themselves." I kept trying to make the marriage work, thinking that was what it meant.

It was a "closet issue" at the time, something that I never heard talked about by anyone. Nor did I read about it. Yes, I was naive. I was terribly ashamed of what had happened in my marriage and I didn't tell anyone—not even my parents.

Seventeen long and painful years later I read a feature article in a major newspaper about abuse. More television news reports followed about separate incidents. Reality reared its ugly head in the public media.

I didn't want the things mentioned in those articles and reports to happen to my family. However, those events brought the topic out of the shadows for me. I learned that a battered wife attempts to leave her abuser seven times before she is successful in getting away. The risk of being killed by the abuser is the greatest during escape attempts.

My husband left the armed services and became a law enforcement officer, which made things more difficult. We lived in an isolated area, even though I begged to live in a populated area. My parents passed away. The same year that I read the newspaper article, 1985, things got so bad that I was concerned that he would kill us and afterward turn the gun on himself. I sought help from a psychiatrist. He said that I needed to get my children and myself to safety as soon as possible. He said that my husband was at a point where he was extremely dangerous, plus he had guns in the house and carried a gun as part of his uniform. He told me that our situation was dire. He referred me to an advocacy center across the state line.

At the advocacy center a counselor by the name of, Diane, helped me to understand the cycle of abuse. I learned that the cycle of abuse was a repeated pattern of built-up of tension, the violence, the apology and promise of the abuser to never do it again.

I told Diane how bad things were at home. I told her that I felt that I was walking on eggshells all the time to avoid the abuse. I explained that every time I got groceries in town with or without the kids along, he accused me of meeting another man and having an affair. She said that we were at an incredibly dangerous point, that we needed to get away from him and to remain safe in the process. I understood that I had to make the decision, but if I tried to escape I needed to bring certain important papers and items that were important to the kids and me. I needed to leave him in complete secrecy because I was in extreme danger. She sent me home with her phone number and more information about abuse, but told me to keep the booklet hidden from my spouse. She warned me that leaving him was the most dangerous time of all for battered women and their children—the time when battered women are most often victimized.

That was the first time I heard how I was labeled, "battered woman" and "victim". I cried when I heard the terms. It was one more step that I took out of the denial that enveloped me for so long. During the next year I learned just how strong denial was and just how strong I was.

I was a member of the Lutheran church. Prayer had always comforted me, but I felt like my prayers were being totally ignored and certainly not answered. It angered me. So, I gave up the effort.

The night after I saw Diane, my husband came home late from work and was crazy drunk. He took his gun and went outdoors in the dark. We heard a gunshot and I told my two children to get down on the floor, out of the light. He fired again. We were so terrified that our teeth chattered. He did not come back into the house for a long time. Did he shoot himself, I wondered? We did not go out to check on him for fear that he would shoot us.

Finally, he returned and accused us of not caring about him at all because we didn't go out to check on him. He put his gun in the gun cabinet and locked it, dished up his evening meal from the cold bowls of food on the table. He walked to the microwave oven, put in his plate and slammed the door so hard that I thought the glass would shatter. I looked up in shock and it was then that I saw the ugly person he had become. It was at that moment I realized that all the love I had ever felt for him was gone. Like all the beauty of a rose, its petals had dried up and fallen away. Love for him simply did not exist anymore. All I felt was terror.

He ate his supper and went to bed with a few choice words directed at me. I could not hear him, but could see his angry face contorted and his mouth moving. What he said to me in anger, I have no idea. I waited until I knew that he was sound asleep before I went to bed. I carefully eased into bed and clung to the edge, as far away from him as possible. Incredibly, I fell asleep even though I was quivering with fear.

Suddenly, I was awakened by a bright light shining in my dresser mirror. I thought it was him playing one of his mean tricks on me. But, I looked across the bed and he was still asleep. I heard a man's voice. The gentle voice invoked trust. The voice said, "Take the children and go." That was all. I was surprised, but I said softly, "I will." The light disappeared.

The next morning my husband left for work. After he left I woke the kids. I explained what we needed to do, how we needed to do it and why. Each of us packed our clothes and chose one thing that was precious to us to bring along. I took the file box and money, as well. We took our cat, abused by him in the past. I left a note telling him that we were gone and would not return. I drove across the state line.

On the way to town, my daughter told me that she had made a plan to go to a swim meet and afterward stay at her friend's house until my son and I got away, too. My son told me that he planned to walk to the fence line and go hand-over-hand and foot-over-foot until he got to a road to run away to a safe place. It was remarkable. Each of us had a plan! Their father passed us on the country road and we waved, but kept moving. He assumed we were going to get groceries.

When I got to town, I stopped at a pay phone and called Diane. She said to meet her at a Chinese restaurant. We succeeded in escaping safely and I got a restraining order, which does not always secure a battered person's safety. He searched for us and asked lots of questions of my friends, but did not find us. He sold all my silver and gold jewelry and a gorgeous silver basket that was my grandmother's silver anniversary gift from my grandfather. I didn't take it with me and I regret it every day. It has never been located, but I won't give up the search

I recall going to the lawyer's office and having to write down the reason for seeking a divorce and having to read it back to him out loud after the secretary had typed it. I was horrified that this was the story of my life. I burst into tears that this was my reality and it was not at all what I had planned for my life or for my children's lives. But there it was--the ugly truth in black and white. The piece of paper in my hands with my own words, broke through the denial. Denial is such a powerful insulator that keeps people from moving beyond hopelessness to freedom from abuse.

People always ask, "Why does a battered woman stay in an abusive marriage?" Then they remark. "I would never put up with that!" I would probably have been one of those who would have felt that way. However, you don't know until you've been there. I believe I stayed because of my religious beliefs, my wedding vows and my desire for my children to not grow up in a broken home—all socially acceptable reasons, aren't they? But then came the abusive treatment; broken promises; shame; denial; covering up the bruises and the truth to family and friends; and the cycle of abuse that worsens with each repetition.

Denial is the main reason victims **stay** in the abuse. Then there are other reasons such as how will they support themselves and their children if they do manage to escape safely; threats from the abuser that he or she will take the children from them and they will never see them again; threats that if "I can't have you no one else can either" meaning they will kill you; and a loss of self-esteem and strength.

I got a divorce and our abuser did not show up in court that day. He knew that he was guilty of the physical abuse he dished out to me and the mental abuse he imposed upon the children and me.

From the moment we escaped, I felt as if there was a giant dome of unbreakable glass over us and that we were protected all the time, but that didn't stop us from being cautious. Was the voice I heard my guardian angel? Did that voice have something to do with the protective dome over us that seemed to insure our safety? I have no doubt that it did. In fact, it must have taken more than one guardian angel to keep us safe during this time.

We survived a horrible and dangerous situation. I was at the absolute weakest point of my life. Diane guided my children and me back to a better place mentally and physically. I felt immense guilt because of a wrong decision in my younger days and then I made the wrong decision to remain in the abusive marriage for so long. The experience damaged our lives. Yes, he made the decision to abuse me and he is responsible for that. It baffles me that he did not assume any guilt. He told his relatives that I was going through my change of life early and was crazy as a result. His family figured out who was really at fault. They called and told me. Later I had to learn about assertiveness and co-dependency before I was able to make any concise change. However, I did make the change back to my former and much happier self.

Recently, I found a copy of a thank you note I wrote to Diane one year and a thousand tears after our escape. It is as follows:

Diane,

Who would have thought that the corner booth at a Chinese restaurant would be the beginning of a new way of life for my children and me? I remember you said, "If we could read the future in the tea leaves, I wonder what we'd see?" Now, nearly one and one-half years later, I can see the difference you have helped to bring about in our lives. I can only speak for myself and how I feel about your work and commitment to my dream.

<u>You</u> held me and let the tears flow, like a turbulent river...

<u>You</u> allowed me to express the pain that made my mind and body ache...

<u>You</u> let me tell you of the ugliness to rid it from within…

<u>You</u> helped to strengthen me when my body shook with fear…

<u>You</u> listened and reflected like a deep and glistening pool…

<u>You</u> cheered me on when I achieved and encouraged me as I struggled…

<u>You</u> challenged me to make decisions and to live with their unknown outcome…

<u>You</u> fostered new growth within me and took time when I felt I deserved none…

<u>You</u> loved me when I didn't even love myself…

<u>You</u> saw beauty in me when I saw only ugliness…

<u>You</u> picked up the pieces of my broken heart and gently helped me heal…

<u>You</u> were patient and kind and did not give up and I'm so very glad!

<u>You</u> made me laugh at my corniness in the middle of my darkest days…

<u>You</u> showed me the way to peace in a violent world…

<u>You</u> gave me so much, not just to me and my children, but to so many others...

The good you do, the love you share and the happiness that evolves because you care are gifts beyond compare. On this day, I dedicate each remaining moment of my future to you because on a day when sunshine was just a memory, I saw a ray of hope in you! Thank you for this and so much more.

Now, thirty years later, I regard my children and myself as survivors. I'm happy and strong. I make better decisions and for that I am glad. I completed my college education and became a social worker. I taught many young people techniques for good decision-making. For my children and me, guardian angels came late, but they did come.

Marilyn V. Davidson

A baby-boomer plus a firecracker, Marilyn Davidson was born on July 4th. Davidson, a native Minnesotan, graduated from Sauk Rapids High School. In her twenties she vacationed out West and was drawn by the beauty of the Big Horn Mountains. She moved there and lives in the Big Horns still.

After raising her children, she graduated with a social work degree from the University of Wyoming. Marilyn shares life with her husband, Roger, a retired college instructor and their boxer, Lars and cat, Sophie. The Davidson's have three children; five grandchildren; and four great-grandchildren.

Watercolor painting, reading, and writing fill Marilyn's free time. Her mother's story-telling of bygone days inspired her love of writing. In warm months Davidson writes on their log home's deck where she is likely to observe wildlife or they observe her. Currently, she is preparing an historical fiction manuscript for publication encompassing the neglected history of the railroad industry's tie hacks.

LONGEST JOURNEY
BY RON L. DOWELL

Before she received the pacemaker to spark her sluggish, eighty-seven year old heart, my mother never liked to exercise. She drove everywhere, even to the corner mailbox, head barely visible above the dash of her ten year old silver Lexus. So after the pacemaker operation, when she complained to her doctor during a routine checkup that she *feels like a chicken with the pip*, he suggested that she, *move about more, hike at a shopping mall, or walk around the block, something not too strenuous, Mrs. Woodson. Exercise some. Or die.*

She's the last living elder. Dad had died from hospital superbug's years back. Grandparents, all uncles and aunts, gone from hypertension, diabetes, or alcoholism. I'd look after Mom, damn it, help kick-start her new lifestyle; keep her healthy and safe, alive longer.

"I clean house every week and push——" She let out a loud breath. "Do you ever push shopping carts at Food4Less?" she grumbled over the phone. "You have to climb over people, crawl under shelves, bag your own stuff. Even Brer Rabbit would have it hard."

A laugh track from a TV show she'd been watching clobbered my eardrum through the receiver.

Why was she so stubborn? "I'm always right about stuff like this, Mom," I said, in my kitchen flipping through a Men's Fitness magazine, the low whir of my Nutri Ninja blender pulverized vegan protein and organic veggies. Some people think I'm strange because I exercise a lot. My sergeant once asked me, *what are you gonna do——die healthy?* Mom never listened, certainly never obeyed. "How can you not know this?" I said.

"Drugstore trips, the bank, washing clothes——that's more than enough exercise for me, Frederick."

Okay, Fred. Don't overreact. She's trying to bait you into giving up. I pushed off the blender, popped a couple of multivitamins and bottomed-up a bottle of bitter lactose-free, sugar-free, and vegan homeopathic anti-anxiety remedy.

"I don't care what Doctor Quack says, I'm not changing. I'll slap taste from his mouth." She must've increased the TV volume or held the phone close to it when the laugh track exploded through the ear piece. "Don't get yourself out of pocket now——you're sixty-five but I'll still take my cane to your butt."

I pulled an ace. "Michelle Obama says everyone needs to get moving."

"No you didn't go there." she said, voice high pitched. "Michelle's my girl——best first lady——right there with Eleanor Roosevelt."

We wrangled, and then she sighed, "Whatever, Frederick. As long as I don't miss my TV shows." She was good for the corner mailbox, about fifteen small boxy homes up the block.

"It can't be too early in the morning——I need my rest, and definitely not after dark in South L.A. I'm old Frederick, and I don't feel safe——hell, between bad cops and thugs, I take my cane everywhere with me."

I worked as parking enforcement officer with the LAPD and this arrangement left a midday half hour between Jeopardy and Judge Judy as best option, fifteen minutes each way to the mailbox and back, enough lunch break for me to rush over in the company Prius with a half hour to spare.

The next day was cloudless, the air crisp, when I arrived in my lime green jogging suit and corn yellow running shoes. Gangsters and cops often made mistakes so I avoided red or blue gang-banger colors. It helps to be seen clearly when jogging through SoLA streets. Built around World War II, her fading periwinkle shotgun corner house faced north. My old bedroom window and the house itself seemed tinier than when I lived there. A shadow line advanced past the porch and flower garden over the yard toward the entry gate. Wind chimes held silent. I bounced ten jumping jacks then fork latched her chain linked fence gate behind me.

Inside, the scent of jasmine touched my nose during Jeopardy's closing credits.

Mom's tight white curls showed beneath her red scarf, black bifocals framed a face that's shaded dark brown and hewn like soft leather. She grabbed her thick wool sweater and cane. The cane's Ebony hardwood was clearly defined throughout, two-toned wood grain Derby handle and shaft. Passed to her down through generations, the collar was made from pewter with delicate flowers and foliage carved into it. There was a steel washer inserted inside the purple rubber tip.

"I've never seen another one like it," she said.

We made for the sidewalk.

Several Latina mothers huddled around a fruit cart on the corner outside the gate. One blinked and said, "Hola Senora!" She touched her throat. "¿Dónde está tu auto?"

Mom flicked her gaze upward toward me. "Garage," she said.

"Are you going for walk? ¿Para caminar?"

"Si. Estoy caminando a mi hijo."

Whatever she said they found funny and they slapped shoulders among themselves. Then the women continued to speak about whatever mothers talk about after they send kids to school.

I spread my legs, squatted, placed my palms to the walkway, and did a few Burpees to warm up. Mom paused for balance, grabbed the right hip that she fell and broke about four years back, as if to align it with the left ankle that she broke seven years ago, when she slipped on wet grass during the college graduation ceremony for my youngest child. We'd ended in emergency surgery just before the commencement speech.

The women cleared a path when Mom tapped a fencepost with her cane. She shaded her eyes, and said, "I never noticed before how far that mail box is."

I barked an order, "Come on Ma, just do it."

She took a deep breath. Camphor tree leaves covered the sidewalk that was buckled from roots. I walked a half step behind, hand on her elbow. She slowed at the sidewalk gradient, wavered but balanced on the cane. Sweat stuck the jogging suit to me, breaths accelerated.

"Hey, Pauline." It was Nosey Rosie the next door neighbor's squawky voice. She was in an orange tunic that was drawn in at her thick waist over black leggings, hair a graying coiled mass that framed her cocoa, moon-shaped face. "I never see you out front. That's a cute sweater——is something wrong with your car?"

"Nawl. Richard Simmons here——," she nods toward me, "thinks I need exercise."

The neighbor rolled her eyes. "Did you know that Mr. Johnson passed?"

Mom stopped mid-stride on the peak of the cracked sidewalk. I held my breath and her triceps. "Oh nawl——I just saw him at Food4Less last week."

I slid in between the two women and did neck rolls to stretch and to refocus Mom away from the neighbor. Rosie folded her arms across her chest. "Keep going mom," I said.

Mom pushed forward off the right foot, two, three feet, over the hump, through loose leaves. *Whew!* She scrunched her face, tapped her cane hard against the concrete, and turned to look around me to Rosie. Her pitch rose, "At the checkout I gave Johnson some coupons for toilet paper."

"He died on the bus stop bench," Rosie said. "Just closed his eyes and never re-opened them."

"Five dollars for three rolls? No way should he pay that," Mom said.

"Only seventy-four, a young man, Pauline. His kids are already fighting over his stuff."

"Full price for toilet paper?" She stroked her forearm in which hand she held the cane, furrowed her eyebrows as if to concentrate. "He'd been a fool to pay it."

"Had just gotten his hair cut too," said the neighbor.

"Humph——they must think we're idiots. Pay that kind of money just to wipe your ass. Might as well use paper money and flush that."

"Funeral's Saturday at Laurel Street MBC, Pauline."

"Nawl."

"Yes, viewing's at ten A.M."

"Seventy-four, you sure? He looked okay to me."

"Ouch," She tapped my shin with her cane shaft.

"He was vegetarian too."

"Mom——Mr. Johnson would've wanted you to keep walking."

"He's dead and you're way too pushy."

"Have you seen Rufus?" Rosie asked. "If you do, send him home. He can't afford no more trouble."

Maybe I was a little aggressive. But ten minutes had passed and we weren't even past the first house. I'd need to shower, change and get back to work.

A few homes later we were in front of Mr. Johnson's house. A big U-Haul mover was backed to the front door. Sure enough, a couple of his children were arguing. A daughter, maybe forty-something, waved.

Mom's mouth turned downward. "Leave the toilet paper." she said. "Show some respect." The woman jumped when mom smashed her cane against the U-Haul hood. "He might need it before he goes through the gates. I tell you as a good Christian."

The woman's head flinched back. She threw a box into the U-Haul, turned away and continued to fuss with her brother over a jewelry box.

Three more houses down a German shepherd snuck up and stuck her big head through space between pickets of a wrought iron fence. Bitch stuck one paw over the horizontal railing, growled like crazy at Mom before I could act. Mom stopped, leaned sideways, wobbled a bit, and then raised her cane high over her head and brought the tip down on the shepherd's nose. She yelped and dashed into the backyard.

The sun was high, air warm. My body weighed down like an anchor dropped in the sea. The exercise thing didn't seem like a good idea for mom. What if she got hurt? I fell to the sidewalk and did twenty pushups. What else could happen?

###

Mom is Great Depression resourceful; clips store coupons, garage full of staples for *the next earthquake.* She'd mastered the art of recycling, removes "lumnum" foil from cooked food carefully, cleans and smoothes it with a dishtowel, and folds it at postal worker speed. Grocery bags and plastic containers received hoarder treatment too.

Halfway to our mailbox rendezvous Homeless Harry shuffled in our direction. "Top of the day to you, Mrs. Woodson. Where's your car?" His gaunt scraggly form blocked the sidewalk; he threw me a sideways look. Crack and weed stink seemed to ooze even from his sidewalk shadow. I held my breath. "Can you spare a quarter?" he said to her. "I'm not doing too great."

"Ass back dude," I said to Harry. "Do we look like welfare to you?"

Mom looked unsteady and Harry touched her shoulder to help stabilize her. "You owe me money," she said to him. "But as a real Christian, I'm gonna forgive you. I've got empty bottles for you at home," she said to Harry. "Worth more than a quarter—— you bag ém———got cardboard and newspaper, some metal scraps too." His shoulders curled forward when she pushed her cane handle into his chest, "I want twenty percent Harry."

Harry quirked an eyebrow and showed beige teeth. "I got yo back, Mrs. Woodson."

"Kick drugs, get in shape dude," I said to Harry. I faked a shoulder punch, he flinched.

"Of course you'll set my trash cans out on Thursday. If you don't, like a good Christian, I'm gonna curb-kick you Harry after I cane-beat you like a runaway slave," Mom said. She flashed a tight grin. The scent from camphor leaves returned once Harry slunk away.

We were maybe fifty feet to the mailbox and a gaggle of young-bloods were shooting dice on the sidewalk, bunched between a white picket fence and overflowed trashcans on the parkway, a bedraggled patch of grass between the sidewalk and curb. They either didn't see us coming or decided to ignore us.

Their clique had on more red colors than bloodshed in a Quentin Tarantino movie. "Whoop——seven eleven got to get to heaven," one said, he crouched with a black wave cap on his head. A forty ounce Olde English 800 malt liquor sweated onto the pavement beside him.

"I got you faded," another said in dark blue Dickies. Pants slung half down his ass, his crimson drawers showed, a red bandana hung from his back pocket.

Their group of six was tight. A couple on their knees I could barely see.

"Excuse us young brothers," I said. They didn't budge and their dice cracked against the concrete.

"You crapped out," said the guy with the red bandana.

Wave Cap had just lost their money. A beefy guy, he stood and twisted his body to face me. Twenty-something, razor bumped coal black face, his voice sounded like a tank rolling across gravel. His eyebrows squished together, top eyelids cut in half his pupils, ripples appeared in his jaw muscles. "You made me lose OG," he said. Top lip turned up, his mouth was full of curses and bitterness. He was in my face and the combined stench of tobacco, weed, and malt liquor reeked from his greasy pores. Fuck. I'd never known anyone in their right mind who could drink that shit and not go stupid. It's said that a good young man can beat a good old man. I'm healthy, he's impaired. I clinched my fist.

"Ahem——," Mom cleared her throat. "Is that you Rufus?" She looked down to a guy still on his knees. His back to us, he picked up loose change. He turned around.

"Oh——what up Mrs. Woodson, where's your Lexus?" He spun a fake gold bracelet that had discolored his amber wrist. Cigarette and weed smoke strangled the air.

"I'm out for a walk, Rosie's looking for you young man." Mom points the purple cane tip at him. "You'd better see what she wants." Rufus nodded his head, waved his arm and the others cleared space for us to continue. "You're on parole. Don't go back to jail. I tell you as the Christian that I am." A flush crept across his light skinned cheeks. "Plus I'll whip your ass with this cane like I used to spank you when you when you were bad."

His partners sniggered.

Rufus straightened his knees. "It's hard, Mrs. Woodson."

"Who told you life is easy?"

He pocketed loose change and trotted home. I released some body tension. We continued our journey.

We reached the mailbox on the corner, Judge Judy started in five minutes, I'd be late back to my job and the sergeant would probably be pissed, overwhelmed with parking violators. Perhaps she'd accept a new exercise routine, maybe not. There's a worldly saying, *nursing the old is like nursing children.* I'd been pretty overprotective. Mom was not yet a child again, nor was my dad, or my grandparents, aunts and uncles. They'd lived their lives as best they could, and when time and circumstance converged, like Mr. Johnson, life ended. Shit, it's God's plan. Other than comfort and unconditional love, there was little else I could give. I'd lower my own pressure with less worry about her.

"Whew," Mom said, "let me rest a minute." She leaned on her cane, one hand on the hot dark blue mailbox. Even in a wool sweater, she didn't sweat at high noon. Not so for me.

"Maybe this wasn't the best idea Mom," I said, mouth dry. "It's taken thirty minutes to reach the corner——you're gonna miss Judge Judy."

Mom squinted. "Oh, didn't I tell you?" She flashed dentures.

"Huh?" My thoughts froze. "Tell me what?"

"Reruns. They're showing Judge Judy reruns Frederick——I've seen it before. Be a good Christian." She handed me keys. "Go, get my car."

Ron L. Dowell

Ron L. Dowell was raised in the Watts and Compton areas of Los Angeles County. In 2008 he retired from a career in healthcare and law enforcement public service with Los Angeles County. He holds three Bachelor's degrees from California State University Dominguez Hills and two Master's degrees from California State University Long Beach. He's a lifetime member of PEN America and, in June 2017, Ron received the UCLA Certificate in Fiction Writing.

Ron is working on *Stones Refused*, a collection of stories that show how people find hope and even joy in lives where basic needs are sometimes hard to meet. His story, *Professor Roach*, will appear in Oyster River Pages, August 2018.

He is a 2018 PEN America Emerging Voices Fellow.

Hocus Pocus
By Jean Ende

Marvin's mother, Elaine, was sick a lot. That's why his aunts frequently took care of him and his sister, Rebecca. Elaine hated the fact that she couldn't care for her own children, but she was glad her sisters-in-law lived nearby and were available. They repeatedly assured her that they didn't mind at all.

Rachel had the easier job. Marvin was 6½ years old, he had big blue eyes and light brown hair and was the best little boy in the whole world. Everyone said so.

"Harvey, your son is no problem at all." That's what Aunt Rachel always told his poppa when she brought Marvin home. "Such a good boy I hardly know he's there. Not like my wild Indians." Aunt Rachel had three sons so she knew what little boys were like

Aunt Helen took care of Marvin's sister who was a teenager and a lot more trouble. Aunt Helen said she had two Sarahs, her own 12-year-old daughter, who was named Sarah, and Rebecca whom she called "Sarah Heartburn" which meant that Rebecca was too dramatic, always carrying on about something. But everyone knew that Aunt Helen didn't really mind.

One day, when Rebecca was younger, she fell off her bike while Aunt Helen was watching her and she wouldn't stop screaming. Her arm and leg were bleeding and Rebecca said she couldn't get up. Aunt Helen ran to the corner and pulled the fire alarm. Rebecca stopped crying and sat up as soon as she heard the siren. The men in the ambulance said it was just a badly scraped knee and elbow and quieted Rebecca with a lollipop and two big bandages with stars on them. They even let her turn the siren on and off.

Aunt Helen was so relieved that she didn't scold Rebecca, and kept hugging and kissing her all the way home. She later told everyone she thought she was going to have a heart attack from all of the commotion.

Marvin liked playing with his older cousins at Aunt Rachel's house where there were lots of toys and always someone to talk with. At his house Rebecca bossed him around because she was older and bigger. And some grown-up was always shushing him if the TV was too loud or he accidently dropped something, reminding him that momma needed her rest. Aunt Rachel was used to noise.

When he was home, Marvin frequently got into bed with momma and she read stories to him. Sometimes Momma told him stories about growing up in Poland where she and Poppa had been born in the same small village although they didn't know each other then. Momma's family ran a business in Poland, Poppa's family spent their days studying with the rabbi. One day bad people came and threatened to harm all of the Jewish people like them, so momma's family and poppa's family had to leave their homes and they all came to New York.

Many of the people from that village settled in the Bronx and that's where Poppa and Momma met and got married. Aunt Rachel's family wasn't from Poland, they were from a place called Lithuania, but the bad people came to her village too so her family also ran away. Aunt Helen was born in America, she had grown up in the Bronx. Both of the aunts eventually met and married Momma's brothers, Marvin's uncles, and now they were all one family and they worked in the same business together.

If his momma was too tired to talk or read stories, Marvin sat quietly in the corner of the bedroom with his crayons and a big pad of paper. He drew pictures of things he made up, pictures copied from the storybooks and pictures of what he thought Momma and Poppa's village looked like

Marvin spent so much time quietly playing by himself that sometimes the grown-ups forgot he was there and he overheard them talking. He didn't understand everything they said, he didn't understand why momma was sick so much, but he understood that she was getting worse and no one knew what to do about it.

***

One day Aunt Rachel took Marvin and her boys shopping and they passed a toy store. Marvin glanced at the window and stopped moving.

"Whatcha lookin' at?" asked his cousin Kenny. "Those baseball gloves are pretty nice, huh? Think you're ready for a big kid's glove?"

Marvin pointed to a big, brightly colored box. "I need that," he said. "Grandma gave me $5 for Chanukah. I have to go home and get my money and buy it. Right now."

Kenny looked at the label on the box. "It's $17.95. You need another $12.95"

Marvin quickly walked over to Aunt Rachel. "Would you give me $12.95?" he asked. "Please?"

Rachel had been watching Marvin and Kenny staring into the toy store, ignoring her, and she had had to call several times before they responded. "I don't have $12.95 to spend on toys," she said. "It's time to go home. No more shopping today. Ask your parents. Maybe you can get it for your birthday."

85

As soon as his poppa got home, Marvin asked to talk to him.

"I've had a long day, Marvin," Harvey said. "Let me wash up and say hello to your momma. We'll talk later."

"I need to talk now," said Marvin.

Harvey smiled at his little boy. Marvin didn't smile back.

Such a serious child, Harvey thought.

"This sounds like an important matter," Harvey said. "Okay. Let's go into the study and talk. Man to man."

Poppa's study was on the ground floor, next to the living room. There was a big desk with a leather chair and walls covered with bookshelves that stretched almost up to the ceiling. Most of the books were in Hebrew, in black leather bindings, many of them looked old.

"I saw something in the toy store that I need to buy," said Marvin. "It costs $17.95 and all I have is the $5 grandma gave me for Chanukah. My birthday is a long time away. Can you give me $12.95? Now?"

"Did you figure out that math by yourself?" Harvey asked.

"No, Kenny told me," said Marvin. "Can you give me $12.95? Please?"

"Well, you're a very focused young man," said Harvey. "You know, money doesn't come easy. I work very hard to earn money for our family's food and clothing, for this house and for all of the toys you already have."

Marvin didn't say anything. He had heard this before.

Harvey thought for a minute, then his face lit up. "You could earn money for your new toy," said Harvey.

"I'm only 6 ½," said Marvin. "I don't have a job."

"Well, I was about your age when I started studying with my father," Harvey said. "I did it because I wanted to be a scholar like him, but for you it's different. I know that. To live in America you need to be able to earn money. That's why I had to give up studying all the time when I came to this country. But maybe you could study with me and make money at the same time. Would you like that?"

Marvin looked at his father skeptically. "What do you mean?"

"I could teach you the Hebrew alphabet. There are 22 letters and every time you learn to write and pronounce a letter properly I'll pay you 15¢. Then we can put the letters together and make words. Each time you learn a word you'll earn 50¢. Pretty soon we'll be able to put the words together and you can recite prayers," said Harvey enthusiastically. He began to talk a little faster and wave his arms.

"You can learn the blessings that should be said at mealtimes and then other blessings. For every blessing you learn by heart you get $1. I haven't bothered to insist on saying these prayers when we eat, that's my mistake. I apologize. Once you know the blessings we'll say them together at each meal. Soon you'll learn other prayers. You can come to the *shul* with me. We can *daven* together. Won't that be fun?" Harvey was smiling, excited.

Marvin hadn't changed his serious expression. "How long will it take to earn $12.95?"

"Ah, your mother's blood is speaking. Focusing on the money not the knowledge," said Harvey. "The men in momma's family, your uncles, have always been merchants, just like they are now. My family was concerned with religion and examining the holy books," said Harvey. "Unfortunately, in America that's not valued so much. The answer depends on you. If you work hard and learn quickly you'll make money quickly. If you don't concentrate it'll take a long time."

Marvin thought it over for a minute.

"You couldn't just give me the money?" he asked.

"I don't think that would be right. It's not fair to your sister for you to get presents for no reason," said Poppa.

Marvin frowned but didn't argue. "Okay," he said. "I'll learn Hebrew."

They planned to start right after dinner.

***

"Maybe you should have just gotten him the toy," said Elaine when Harvey told her about the arrangement. "He asks for so little. Rebecca is always carrying on and gets a lot more than he does. What does he want so badly?"

"Who knows? What does it matter? Probably a ball or a bat or something for baseball. I hear the men talking about the ballgames all day long in the shop," said Harvey. "No, this is the best way. I'll study with my son, just like my father studied with me. He'll realize how rewarding it is. Once he has the baseball glove, or whatever it is he wants, I'm sure he'll want to continue studying."

Harvey began to laugh. "An American *tsaddik,* a scholar who is knowledgeable about baseball and holiness."

***

Marvin and Harvey worked together every evening after dinner. Harvey was disappointed that Marvin didn't exhibit more of a facility for learning Hebrew, but he tried to be patient, impressed by his son's determination. He was confident that Marvin would soon catch-on and start to love this work. Their study time was the high point of Harvey's day. He began humming long forgotten Hebrew melodies to himself while he drove to and from work.

"I haven't seen Harvey so happy since I got sick," Elaine told Rachel. "He's really enjoying these lessons. I just hope he's not working Marvin too hard."

Learning Hebrew was more difficult than Marvin had anticipated. He already knew his ABCs in English and didn't understand why he needed another alphabet. But he kept at it until he knew all of the letters and their sounds. Memorizing prayers was a lot harder. Marvin's cousins, who were older and therefore preparing for their Bar Mitzvahs at Hebrew school, offered to help.

"It's a regular yeshiva in my house these days," reported Rachel. "Harvey, whatever you're paying Marvin, I should reimburse you double as thanks for getting them all to keep quiet for a while and stop tearing up the house."

Harvey paid promptly. Each time Marvin mastered something new the money was placed in a cigar box Marvin got from the local candy store. Every night, before he went to sleep, Marvin carefully counted his cash. It took him two months to earn all of the money he needed.

"Will you take me to the mall tomorrow poppa?" Marvin asked as soon as he deposited the final coins in his box. "It's Thursday tomorrow. The store stays open late on Thursday. We can go when you come home from work."

"Okay, my scholar," said Harvey. "I'll try to come home early."

"And don't tell momma that I've gotten all of the money I need," said Marvin. "I want it to be a surprise."

"I know she's proud that you're earning your own money for your toy and she'll be impressed by how much Hebrew you've learned," said poppa. "You know there's lots more to learn. Would you like to continue our lessons?"

Marvin looked at poppa. "I have enough money," he said. "I don't need any more lessons."

"Maybe you'll change your mind when you're a little older," said Harvey.

***

When they got to the toy store Harvey was surprised to see Marvin run past the display of baseball equipment to the boxed games. "That's it," said Marvin. "That's what I want. It's still here. I was afraid someone else would buy it."

He was pointing to a large red and gold box. On the cover, in big silver letters, were the words, I CAN DO MAGIC. The young boy on the box was wearing a black cape and tall black silk hat and holding a black wand. There was a tail of bright, multi-colored stars on the wand's gold tip.

"You need a magic set?" said Harvey.

"I need it for momma," said Marvin. "I need it right away. I can't reach it. Get it for me. Please poppa, reach it for me."

Harvey got the toy and handed it to Marvin. "You're going to put on a magic show for momma?" he said. "That's what all of the fuss is about? She likes magicians? I never knew. Well, I'm sure she'll enjoy your show."

Marvin didn't hear his father, he had already run to the cashier and was carefully counting out his money. He grabbed the box from the clerk as soon as the transaction was over.

"Now, let's go home," he said to poppa.

As soon as they got into the house, Marvin went to the study and tore the cellophane wrapping off his magic kit. He opened the box and stared at the contents, confused. Under the collapsible hat and the cape and instruction sheet were a bunch of cellophane bags, bags with rings, paper flowers, small scarves and other items that made no sense to Marvin.

"Let me help you," said Harvey. "This is really a toy for a little older child, I'll show you how it works."

Harvey read the instructions to himself carefully while Marvin squirmed and then his poppa started explaining how to do the tricks. "See," he said. "These rings have very thin cracks, you can barely see them. Just tell people they're solid, wave your wand, and say hocus pocus. Then you bang them together at just the right spot and they join, you can make a chain. And this wire lets you hide the colored scarfs in your sleeve so you can pull them out and surprise people. The main thing is to keep talking and move quickly, wave the wand around and get people to look the other way so they can't figure out what you're doing."

Marvin looked at Poppa. He looked at the contents of the box. He looked at the illustrations on the direction sheet. **"THAT'S NOT MAGIC! THAT'S JUST TRICKING PEOPLE!"** Marvin yelled. **I WANTED MAGIC!**

Harvey had never heard Marvin yell so loudly. "Calm down," he said. "What's the problem? Of course it's tricks. What did you think it was? If you practice and do the tricks well you'll look like a real magician."

Marvin picked up the box, held it as high as he could and threw it to the ground. "I don't need tricks. I need magic," he screamed. Marvin jumped on the box again and again and again. "I need magic to make momma not sick anymore."

He kicked the box so hard it flew across the floor and crashed into the wall. Rings and scarfs and flowers and glitter scattered all over. Marvin ran over to the box and jumped on it again and again. Then he kicked it again and the box crashed into another wall.

Marvin was crying. His nose was running. "Momma has been sick too much. I wanted to make her better."

"Oh Marvin, my poor little boy." Harvey got on his knees and put his arms around Marvin until he stopped sobbing. Harvey went into the bathroom and got a glass of water and a tissue for his son.

"I know it's hard to have momma be so sick," Harvey said. "But there's no magic cure. The doctor is doing all he can to help momma get better."

"The doctor can't do anything more," said Marvin. "I heard him say so."

"You hear so much don't you?" said Harvey. "You sit there quietly, looking so busy while the grown-ups talk. I'm sorry we don't notice you, there are things you shouldn't hear, things that you can't understand."

Harvey got up and walked over to the bookshelf. He pulled out one of his books, it had Hebrew words printed in gold on the cover. "The doctor is still working hard to cure momma and meanwhile we can do our part and pray for her. The Lord is more powerful than any doctor, than any medicine, than any magic trick.

Harvey opened the book to a page in the middle. "Look here," he said. "This is a prayer to ask for help for a sick person, to ask that their pain is eased, and they regain their health. You already know many of these words, I'll help you with the others. Would you like to say it with me?"

Marvin blew his nose and squinted his eyes hard. He glared at Harvey. "You pray all the time. I've heard you reading these books in the morning and at night. It doesn't do any good," he yelled. "This is just like the magic game."

Marvin grabbed the book out of poppa's hand and threw it down. Then Marvin kicked it so hard the book flew across the floor just like the magic kit did. He ran over and jumped on the book and the spine broke.

Harvey ran across the room, his face red, his eyes bulging. He was screaming Hebrew and Yiddish words that Marvin had never heard. He grabbed Marvin by the arm and lifted him off the ground. Harvey was a big man, Marvin was a small boy. Harvey could hold Marvin high above the floor and dig both hands into Marvin's shoulders. He shook Marvin. Once, and then again.

"No poppa, no," Marvin yelled.

Harvey froze. He looked into Marvin's eyes, then he pulled his small boy into his own large chest and put him down carefully. "I'm sorry," said Harvey. "Are you okay? I didn't mean to hurt you."

Marvin nodded but didn't say a word.

Harvey picked up the Hebrew book, examined the ripped spine, kissed the book quickly and put it back on the shelf.

Marvin was quiet. He was shaking a little, still crying, and his nose was running again. The places on his shoulders where poppa had held him up in the air and squeezed him, hurt, but Marvin didn't touch them. He just sat quietly on the floor.

"You know it's a sin to mistreat a holy book. It's called a desecration, that means a terrible sin," Harvey said. "Many bad people have destroyed Jewish books. Just like they tried to destroy the Jewish people. That's why I got so upset. But you're a child, you didn't know what you were doing. I'm sorry that I forgot that, sorry that I scared you."

"I'm okay poppa," said Marvin. "I'm sorry I hurt your book."

***

Rebecca and Elaine were upstairs in their bedrooms. Rebecca was simultaneously doing her homework, talking to a friend on the phone and listening to the radio. She vaguely heard the noise downstairs and ignored it. Elaine was in bed, dozing. It took her a while to wake up and identify the noise.

She could tell that Marvin was in pain and Harvey was yelling. Elaine called out. Harvey and Marvin didn't hear her, but Rebecca rushed into her mother's room.

"Help me get downstairs," Elaine demanded.

"I'll go find out what's going on," Rebecca said. "You stay here."

"No, I want to see for myself," said Elaine. "I just need a little help."

They arrived in the study to find Marvin sitting on the floor, Harvey standing over him. Pieces of the magic kit were scattered all over the room. Glittering strings that had been attached to the wand had broken off and there were sparkles on the bottom of Harvey's pants. Marvin was absently wiping his nose with a multi-colored silk scarf.

"What did you do to him?" Rebecca yelled at Harvey. She ran to her brother.

"What's going on here?" said Elaine softly. "Are either of you hurt?"

Harvey and Marvin explained what had happened

"You goofball," Rebecca said to her brother. She was sitting on the floor with her arm around Marvin's shoulder.

Having Rebecca's arm resting where Poppa had grabbed him hurt a little, but Marvin didn't mind.

"You really thought you were going to yell, "Hocus Pocus" and everything would be okay? You're really a jerk. You know that?"

Marvin smiled at her and nodded.

"Come here, all of you," said Elaine. She was sitting on the couch. Harvey sat down on one side of her, Marvin on the other. Rebecca sat next to Marvin.

Elaine looked from Harvey to Marvin. "You both were trying to do a good thing, but it didn't work out the way you wanted it to. It's no one's fault," she said. "There's no reason to be mad. I love all of you."

Elaine hugged Harvey and then she hugged Marvin and Rebecca and sent them upstairs. When she put her arm around Marvin, he winced, and Elaine pulled his polo shirt away from his shoulder and saw the bruises on her son's arms and shoulders.

It'll take a while for those to fade, Elaine thought. Rachel will see the bruises when Marvin is rolling around with her boys. I'll have to explain before she asks Marvin what happened.

Rebecca went to Marvin's room with him. They sat on the floor and played three games of checkers and she let Marvin win all of them. When he changed into his pajamas she saw the bruises on her brother.

"Did Poppa do that to you?"

"Yes, he was mad because I hurt his book,"

"That's not such a terrible thing, and anyway you didn't mean it," said Rebecca. "He should pick on someone his own size."

"Don't say anything, Rebecca," said Marvin. "I don't want anyone to be mad anymore."

"Don't worry, I won't do anything now, it would just upset momma," said Rebecca. "But someday. Someday when I'm older."

***

The next day, the aunts came to visit and Elaine told them what had happened.

"Before you start, I'm telling you, don't say a bad word about Harvey," Elaine said. "He's Marvin's father, he loves him. You don't know what he endured in Poland.

"For him it was worse than what you went through," she said to Rachel who had left Europe before Elaine's family did.

"Far worse than what you heard about in America," she said to Helen.

"He's a good man, but he'll need your help when I'm gone."

Helen and Rachel started to tell her not to talk like that, that she'd recover soon. But Elaine cut them off.

"Medicine is not going to cure me. Prayers are not going to cure me. Now I see that even a magic wand cannot cure me. I'm ready. But for me to go in peace you have to promise you'll both watch out for my children."

Helen and Rachel nodded.

The three women joined hands and cried softly.

###

Jean Ende

Jean Ende is a nice Jewish girl from the Bronx who moved to Brooklyn and is trying to exorcize her background by writing about her immigrant family. Her stories have appeared in *Stories That Need to be Told, Bosque Magazine, Poets and Dreamers, Jewish Literary Review, University of California Press and JewishFiction.net*. A graduate of the City College of New York, Jean worked as a newspaper reporter, political press secretary, and publicist for non-profit agencies before going over to the dark side, getting an MBA from the Columbia University Graduate School of Business, and working as a marketing executive and college business professor. Since retiring she's taken writing courses with the Stonybrook University MFA program, and has been admitted to the Breadloaf writing conference three times. Jean is almost finished with her first novel.

Dubs Secret
By Rick Forbess

Shortly after meeting Lummy at Blackwell's Crossing, Dub transferred the leg, wrapped in a green wool army blanket, to the trunk of his car. He had arrived an hour after dark, and except for the sound of the stream's lazy flow over the road crossing, it had been quiet. Now lightning flashes in the north preceded booming thunder, and a cooling breeze was picking up. He closed the trunk and turned to see Lummy standing in silhouette, calf deep in the middle of the crossing, smoking a cigarette, and facing upstream.

"Lummy. What's going on? What are you doing out there?"

There was no answer, but Dub heard a faint humming sound, or thought he did, coming from the direction Lummy was looking.

"You're ruining your boots," Dub said.

The humming again; this time there was no doubt, and within just a few seconds it sounded like a muffled growl. Dub thought he heard rifle shots punctuating the roar, but how could there be so many, and getting closer so quickly?

"Goddamn it, Lummy."

By the time Dub realized what was about to happen, he had just enough time to jump in his car and fish tail back up to the crest of the road before the flash flood, choked with trees and limbs, rumbled through the crossing.

Lummy's pickup truck had been parked on the other side of Little Mud Creek just a few feet from the water's edge. Dub didn't really expect to see Lummy when he looked back, but he was shocked that his truck was gone. He pulled a flashlight from the glove compartment and swept the beam downstream. There it was, rolled over on its side 150 feet from the crossing, pinned against two boulders, water rushing around both ends. Most of the chassis was underwater, but the driver's side wheels and edge of the frame along that side were visible. He yelled out for Lummy, but there was no answer. He ran down as close as he dared and yelled again, over and over as loud as he could. He stepped into the edge, only ankle deep, but slipped right away. He braced the fall with his left arm and struggled to regain his footing, slipping once more, but in deeper water this time, before he managed to get back to dry land. He sat down on an old tree stump and then stood right back up to walk a few feet along the edge of the water in the direction of Lummy's pickup. He stopped and quieted his breathing so he could listen. He yelled for Lummy, but heard only the sound of the rushing water. By quick reckoning, he decided that it would be best to leave and keep quiet about the whole thing. He knew he couldn't help Lummy, and he'd have to lie if questioned about why he was there and what he'd seen.

***

Dub drove the farm to market roads for a couple of hours before he headed back to his house. *Lummy, what happened? Why did you just stand there like you didn't care, almost like you wanted it to happen? Lord have mercy.*

Rather than park out front on the street when he got home, Dub pulled around the corner and edged up into his back yard next to the shed. He locked the trunk and slipped in the back door, through the kitchen. He put his still damp clothes in the hamper and got into bed next to Dorothy, who didn't stir.

He didn't sleep, but the next morning he was up early, as usual, and stuck to his routine of brewing coffee and sipping the first cup while listening to the farm and cattle report on the radio. When the news came on, he turned the volume down and leaned over the table with his ear next to the speaker. Rain totals from the storm was the lead story and then a small fire at the cotton gin, the fire chief's retirement, Spruce Up Day at the cemetery, and another hot one forecast, but nothing about

Lummy. He turned the radio up a bit for the gospel hour and silently prayed. During "Take My Hand Precious Lord" and "How I Got Over" he hummed along with the melodies.

When Dorothy came into the kitchen, she asked him how he had slept and if he'd caught any fish. For several nights lately, he'd left just after supper to go run his trotlines while there was still some light. Most nights he came home with at least one nice sized catfish and would usually skin, gut, quarter the fish and put it in the icebox to soak in milk until it was fried the next night. Dub replied that the only thing he'd hooked was a cottonmouth, and he had cut its head off before removing the hook.

"One less snake," Dorothy commented. "What time did you get in anyway? I woke up once and it was almost 11:00."

"It was pretty late, after midnight. After I ran the line, I sat out there quite a while trying to catch something on the rod and listening to the thunder. Must have been a heck of a storm over in Brown County. Got a couple of bites, but that's it. Managed to trip though, and got all wet, but I just kept with it for a while."

"Honey, you always was hopeful. That's one thing I love about you," Dorothy replied. She poured herself a cup of coffee and then started frying the bacon and eggs.

***

On the drive to the brickyard after breakfast Dub thought about the long day ahead of him and wondered if he'd be able to pull it off. It would be hard to go about business as usual knowing Lummy would never be there again. He didn't like to think about where Lummy actually was, but he couldn't get his mind off it. *What were his last thoughts? Who would find him? Would they lay him out on the bank of the creek and just stare at his face? I guess he's in heaven now.* He lived alone, so someone would have to come along and see the pickup to even know there was a problem. Of course the brickyard would notice that he didn't show up for work, but how long before they'd try to contact him?

He'd worked with Lummy for nine years and couldn't remember a day he'd not shown up. They were the only two burners and shared the responsibility of tending to the four kilns. They worked with a quiet, synchronized efficiency that the forklift operators, clay mixers, and molders envied and resented. Dub was a big cut up, and even though Lummy was five years younger, he was more serious in both countenance and demeanor. Despite the differences in personality, they were more comfortable in each other's company than with anyone else.

Not fifteen minutes after starting work, Willy Merryman, the kiln boss, asked Dub if he'd seen Lummy.

"No, I ain't. Maybe you should send somebody to go by his house. He might be sick or something," Dub said. Then he turned away to look into the kiln like he was checking on how the bricks were baking.

"We can't afford to lose another man just to drive over there. You'll have to handle the kilns until he shows up. We got four ton to finish by noon."

It was a long morning, but Dub managed to keep up with the work pretty well even though his heart wasn't in it. At noon he sat alone in the shade of a mesquite tree next to the parking lot where he and Lummy usually had lunch together. They had developed a routine of swapping items from their pails; one of Dorothy's egg burritos spiced up with hot sauce for a couple of Lummy's Ding-Dongs, or a home baked biscuit with sausage for a slice of Lummy's bread pudding. They pretty much knew what each other liked, and the lunches were prepared for the other as much as themselves. They rarely talked about work, and rather than the hard-edged kidding and sex jokes that were typical among the other men, they talked about themselves; their childhoods, their favorite country western singers, their beliefs about various Bible verses. Now Lummy was gone. It still didn't seem real, but Dub knew things would never be the same, and he put a good bit of the blame on his own shoulders.

Dorothy had packed a ham sandwich, potato chips, a slice of coconut cream pie, and a thermos of cold sweet tea, but Dub didn't have an appetite, so he only nibbled on the sandwich and drank some of the tea. Like she often did, Dorothy had included a note folded and sitting on top of the lunch. "Save room for fried chicken at supper. Love, Dot." Dub knew he was a lucky man to have Dorothy. She had saved him from the honky tonk life of his younger years, and was the most tenderhearted and loving person he'd ever known.

Sitting there, Dub thought about lunch a week earlier when Lummy asked, "You ever heard the story of the old woman's leg and her ghost?"

"Yeah, I heard of it," Dub replied. "How come? You seeing ghosts?"

"Not yet, but I got that leg," Lummy replied.

"Come on, Lummy. You ain't kidding me are you?"

"No. I ain't."

Like most grownups in their neighborhood, Dub had heard the leg story several times over the years. As most often told, an elderly woman was murdered by her husband during the depression. The day before the couples' cows and pigs were to be shot and buried in long trenches by government men, the husband went clean off his rocker. After he clubbed and dismembered his wife, he filled the pockets of his overalls and coat with rocks, walked into the livestock tank, and drowned. Her left leg had never been found, and her ghost, fully formed except for the missing leg, wandered around the countryside at night looking for it, often floating across bodies of water.

"I've never told anybody about this, Dub, and it's not a jokey thing. Are you sure you want to hear it?"

"Yeah, I guess so, Lummy. I mean, why not."

"Okay. I just want you to know that I got a really, really big favor to ask, but you don't have to do it if you don't want to. I just want to be clear about that from the beginning."

"Alright, Lummy. What is it", Dub asked. Lummy's goofy smile had given way to a serious, studious look, like he was trying to solve a math problem.

The way Lummy spoke, slowly and to the point in his high-pitched voice, left people with the impression that he wasn't much of a thinker, but Dub knew better and listened carefully. Lummy explained that since shortly after the woman's death twenty years ago, the leg had been passed from one man to another and that it had been in his care for a year. His mission was to restore the leg to the woman's ghost so she could find peace, but it would happen only if the leg was kept whole and brought to bodies of water between dusk and dawn to wait for her spirit to find it. These men knew what they were doing would be judged as sacrilege by most, so they took an oath on the Holy Bible to keep their names and what they were doing secret except for those who each man selected as next in line.

"Dub, I'm asking you, as my best friend in the world, to take this over for me. I'm just worn out over it. I can't take it no more. If you decide you can't, then I won't think no less of you. I don't want to do anything to make you turn against me."

They were sitting cross-legged, so close to each other that the soles of their work boots almost touched, but each was looking straight ahead, staring into the distance. A few seconds passed before Dub said anything, and when he did it was in a voice so quiet Lummy had to lean in to hear. "Lummy, if you want me to, I'll do it, but I don't think no ghost is coming for that leg, and this all goes against God's word."

***

On the drive home after work, Dub stopped at the bait shop to buy two dozen minnows for his trotline. As usual, the radio sitting next to the cash register was on.

"The Guttman County Sheriff's Department reports that a local man is feared drowned. At approximately 7:45 AM this morning, a Flat Plains School District bus driver noticed an overturned pickup truck resting several yards downstream from Blackwell's Crossing on Little Mud Creek in Brown County. The severe thunderstorms that hit the area last night caused flashfloods in several smaller creeks, including the Little Mud. A coordinated search downstream from Blackwell's Crossing began before noon today, but at the time of this broadcast, Mr. Barnett had not been found.."

Mrs. Toom, lit cigarette dangling from her lips while she scooped up the minnows from the holding tank, slowly shook her head from side to side.

"I bet he's drowned and washed up somewheres way downstream. I only knowed him as a customer, but he seemed like a nice man to me. Did you know him?"

Dub looked away to answer. "Not really, tell you the truth. We worked together up at the brickyard, but really, we didn't talk much."

He parked next to the shed out back again when he got home, and sat for a few minutes trying to sort things out. *What a goddamn nightmare this is and all because of a stupid leg and a bunch o' stupid ole boys who believe in ghosts. Lummy, why did you have to get involved? Jesus don't believe in ghosts, even if his disciples did, and the Bible says that when a person dies, the soul and spirit go right to heaven or hell. This could be God's wrath right here. Hell, it could be for all I know. What am I gonna do with that damn leg? Carry it around in my trunk forever? That ain't gonna do Lummy no good, and I could end up just like him.*

He saw Dorothy open the back door and call out, "Dub. Dub. Come on in, honey. What are you doing out there?"

He grabbed his lunch pail from the seat next to him, got out, and walked up to the door where she was still standing.

As soon as they stepped inside the kitchen, Dorothy hugged him tightly. "What's wrong, honey?"

Dub, stiffened for a couple of seconds, and then relaxed. "I'm okay, but I just heard that Lummy Barnett got washed away in a flashflood. They ain't found his body yet though."

"Oh, I'm so sorry. That's horrible. When did it happen?"

"According to the news it was last night," Dub replied.

Dub had come up with a plan for the leg while sitting in the car. He would leave it near, but not too near, where he put his boat in to run the trotline on Jim Ned Creek, ridding himself of the thing and honoring Lummy at the same time. He sat down to supper feeling a measure of relief, but it didn't last long.

"Honey, why don't I go with you tonight to run the trotline?" Dorothy asked. "It's so cool out there of an early evening, and I haven't been out there in a while."

"You'd miss your show, Dot. Ain't 'I Married Joan' on tonight, and running the line may be a waste of time."

"Yeah, but I won't miss that silly show much, and I'd rather spend the time with you," Dorothy replied.

"Okay, then. Let's be sure to take your lawn chair. I'll take an extra flashlight too, just in case."

***

They arrived a few minutes before sunset, and by the look of things, the thunderstorms had missed the Jim Ned watershed. Dub's boat was still chained to the tree next to the bank and looked undisturbed since his last time there two nights earlier. The wind was calm and the mirrored surface of the stream pool looked almost completely still. It was quiet except for the deep throated croaking of bullfrogs from the near distance and the sound of the crickets' rhythmic chirping closer at hand.

While Dub fumbled with the boat, Dorothy carried her chair a few yards downstream to her customary spot. The ground there was flat, and an opening in the trees and bushes along the bank gave her a nice view of the stream flowing out of the pool. She wasn't able to watch Dub run the trotline from there, but if he caught anything he always yelled out to let her know.

Once he was sure Dorothy was settled in, Dub turned the boat over and put the paddles in, but left it chained to the tree and partially in the water. He lifted the bucket of minnows from the backseat floorboard and carried it down to the bank where he left it sitting in the boat. Then he went back to the car, quietly opened the trunk, and picked up the leg, which was still wrapped in the green wool army blanket.

He had already selected a place to leave the leg and was sure he could make it there and back before Dorothy would recognize that he was slower than normal running the line. About fifty yards upstream the creek narrowed to fifteen feet in width before flowing into the pool. Access to the spot was fairly easy; just squeeze through the bushes and scramble down a two-foot high bank. The spot was level and grassy on both sides, and the stream was usually shallow enough for a dry crossing by stepping from one of the big rocks breaking the surface to another.

A couple of minutes after leaving with the leg, Dub made it to the grassy bank. He was a bit winded, but felt confident about being able to get back well before Dorothy become suspicious. He knelt and carefully placed the leg, still wrapped in the blanket, on the ground. His thoughts were about Lummy and about how proud of himself he was for honoring his dearest friend in this way. Since he'd never seen the leg, the thing that had led to Lummy's death, he decided to take a look. Carefully, he pulled back the corners and edges of the blanket. The light of dusk was beginning to fade by then, so he used his flashlight to get a clear look.

What Dub saw was disgusting. *This ugly thing is what Lummy died for?* The leg was bent at the knee at a sixty-degree angle. Long, yellowed nails curled over the end of withered toes. Reddish-brown skin, dry as leather, stretched tightly over foot, ankle, shin, and thighbone. *Sweet Jesus in heaven. Forgive him.*

Dub whispered a prayer, but after a few seconds opened his eyes when he noticed that the bullfrogs and crickets had gone quiet. There was no breeze, and the stream's bubbly flow came to an abrupt standstill.

Across the stream, a faint shadow seemed to move in the gathering darkness among the trees. Dub leaned forward and squinted into the deepening shade to get a better look. At first he detected nothing, but then the shadow, now more distinct in form, moved forward and stopped just on the edge of the tree line. He clearly saw the outline of a woman wearing a long dress. Color and texture filled the outline from bottom to top like water rising in a clear glass. The woman wore a dress of dark color, maybe purple or black. She stared directly into his eyes without expression. What appeared to be a large smudge or bruise, it was hard to tell in the fading light, spread from her left temple to jawline.

"Evenin'," Dub said.

The woman's lips moved, but there was no sound.

"Ma'am, are you okay?" Dub asked, almost whispering.

She continued mouthing silently and slowly raised her left arm to point directly at the leg lying on the ground in front of Dub.

Dub looked down to the leg and then back to the woman. She was closer now, standing on a rock in the middle of the stream. Dub shined his flashlight down to help her see where to step next. From the bottom of the dress only one ankle and foot, the right one, stood on the rock.

Dub starred at the ankle and foot for a couple of seconds while holding the flashlight a little higher and squinting to get a better look. The woman was standing on one leg. Without moving the leg, she moved forward again, floating and then hovering just above the stream between the rock and Dub's side of the creek.

"Oh," Dub gasped, and his right arm jerked back, sending the flashlight flying as he fell backwards. He turned and crawled as fast as he could toward the bank. He tried to stand but fell and then crawled again until he finally made it through the thick bushes to the clearing. He stood and ran back toward the car, but almost there, saw Dorothy standing in the path, so he slowed as much as he could and did his best to keep his composure.

"Honey, how did you cut your cheek? Where's your flashlight?" Dorothy asked.

Dub quickly glanced back over his left shoulder. "Branches," Dub replied.

"Branches? Where did you go? Did you run the line?"

"I went to see if they was any minnows schooling at that little place where the stream runs into the pool. I tripped and dropped the flashlight in. Let's just go home, Dot. I don't feel good."

"Sure, honey, you want me to take care of the boat?" she asked.

Dub said he'd do it, and as Dorothy shined her flashlight down to the edge of the water, he hurried to pull the boat back up, flipped it over, and poured the minnows into the creek. Dorothy asked to drive home, and this time Dub let her.

When Dorothy pulled out on the main road, she turned on the radio. Ray Price was singing "Crazy Arms", one of Dub's favorites, but he didn't hum and sing along like usual.

Just minutes from home, the top-of-the-hour news opened with the lead story. "The man reported missing earlier today and feared caught in a flash flood last night on the Little Mud Creek, forty-three-year-old Lummy Barnett of Guttman, has turned up alive."

"Oh, my, God. What a blessing. Dub, can you believe it?

Rick Forbess

Rick Forbess immigrated from Texas to Maine in 1980, where he still lives happily with his wife of forty-five years. He's an emerging writer with four previously published short stories and a long list of rejections. As his long career in the mental health field winds down, he's devoting time to learning the craft of writing fiction. It has been a humbling and gratifying experience.

Monterey Papa
By Debbie Fowler

Hildy adjusted her monitor so she could see it from a slouched position in the desk chair. She would have aching neck muscles again tonight but her assignment would run on the evening news and couldn't be done leisurely. She sipped her iced coffee and hit the play button on the third disc of *The Complete Monterey Pop Festival.*

Hooch Conrad had died the night before and Hildy's task was to piece together the few public glimpses of his professional life for the requisite video homage. Even though Hooch only had one . . . no, two Top 40 hits in the late sixties. Though he was best remembered for eccentric mug shots, one where he'd held up two fingers in a droopy, druggy peace sign. Even though he hadn't been on the public scene for thirty years, he'd still get a tribute. The Baby Boomers from her parents' generation in the TV audience ate that stuff up and asked for seconds.

At that groundbreaking concert in Monterey, California, circa 1967, Hooch attained notoriety partially because he left the stage without finishing his Number One Hit from that year, *Radio*

Peace. To the audience it appeared that he thought he was done when he took an abrupt bow, mid chorus, and left the stage. His ironically titled second release, *Not Enough*, never climbed higher than number twelve on the charts. Denied the important sophomore hit, he faded away into that obscurity reserved for those who had glittered only briefly in the fickle spotlight. He'd pop back up every few years with a misdemeanor or felony, do his time, and slip back into whatever.

'*Whatever*' apparently caught up with the sad old rocker last night. His nephew found him unconscious and the EMT's were not able to revive him. No exotic or legendary exit for Hooch - it was apparently a massive stroke. Cremation was scheduled for later that day and it was buzzed throughout social media that his ashes were to be auctioned off online. Creepy.

Hildy wasn't yet born when California's 1967 Monterey Pop Festival was staged, so she was unfamiliar with the concert, even if she did know about many of its stars. She and her friends were big fans of the Grateful Dead, the Who, and Janis Joplin - both in and out of Big Brother and the Holding Company. Hildy assumed she'd get a kick out of the concert footage of those favorites, but was surprised at how much she was getting into the entire production. Maybe she was becoming a connoisseur of music. She even liked some of the Blues. She might play The Paul Butterfield Blues Band for her friends. Could be there *was* something significant about this golden assembly of rockers from the pivotal era leading up to Woodstock. Millions of Baby Boomers may not be wrong.

It was easy to see from the concert tape that the audience certainly believed something awesome was taking place. Candidly caught on film while history occurred on stage, some spectators were in worlds of their own making, some swayed, some rocked hard. Hildy was captivated by the hairstyles, makeup, sunglasses and fashions, how relatively organic these young people appeared, caught on film in unstaged leisure. They seemed soft and genuine — less slick, hard and cynical than today's kids. A dichotomous reaction when one recalled that the Boomers' generation became famous for its mass mutiny against status quo.

Hildy wondered what was going on in the thoughts of these kids as they sat en masse on the cusp of societal change. The world was a vastly different place in 1967 from the perspective of the 21st Century. Who could've known the future of rock and roll? Who could've guessed the outcome of the burgeoning anti-war, civil-rights, women-are-people-too awareness from the turbulent mid-century? Hildy decided to follow up on these questions by talking with her mother — if not a radical participant then certainly an eye-witness.

The Mamas and the Papas were treating her to their distinctively sweet harmony when she sensed a morsel of recognition in a passing shot of the audience. The camera focused on a girl who had been in several previous shots, probably because she was very cute — long straight, bangless hair, her left cheek painted with the words *PS I LUV YOU*. A continuous smile on her face, she lip-synced the lyrics and was obviously very tuned in to the concert vibe. But Hildy didn't know this girl from the man in the moon; she was more interested in a guy behind and to the smiling girl's right.

She hit the short reverse and sent Mama Cass back a verse. Then she sat up straight to better view the impending crowd scene. There! She froze the picture and inched it back, back, back until just before the man came into three-quarter view. Then she played the five second scene at several speeds. The LUV girl partially blocked him, but Hildy was very nearly convinced that she was looking at a video image of her father from 1967!

***

Two hours later, the newsroom editor stood, straightening her impossibly curled body. She found her right leg pins-and-needles numb. If Hildy didn't take a break she was afraid the image of the corrugated awnings from the mid-century Monterey fairgrounds might get permanently burned into her subconscious. She'd torn herself away from this greedy new quest for more glimpses of her late father to finish the film clip on Howard "Hooch" Conrad. The scene of his premature exit from the concert stage was added to the ubiquitous mug shots and the exterior takes of the ambulance leaving the dead rocker's Pasadena residence. Hildy pronounced the assignment completed. Her overused brain cells conjured a goofy thought about the planned memorial service for Hooch — wouldn't it be funny if everyone left the ceremony before it was concluded.

Her parallel personal project was shaping up. She'd found two more snippets of the man in the crowd and one more possible shot as he walked in slow motion through a large open area where concert-goers lounged freely. She was convinced that she was actually viewing David Fallon at the age of nineteen. She decided to keep the disks out instead of relegating them to storage in order to review the bookmarked segments later.

***

The next day, on a visit with her mother, Hildy announced a surprise. Debbie complimented her daughter's work on the Hooch Conrad piece from the news. It had been replayed on the local morning wake-up show and when Debbie spoke to several of her friends that day she'd proudly announced that her daughter was the "artist" who put the piece together. Hildy reminded her mom for the umpteenth time that she was more engineer than artist, but Debbie's parental concept remained unaltered.

Hildy set up the DVD and positioned the laptop so both she and her mother could see the screen. The edited scenes played through but Debbie made no comment, no change in her facial expression of unfulfilled anticipation, no sign that she saw anything that Hildy had expected.

"You didn't see anyone familiar?" Hildy asked in disbelief.

"No, I don't think so. Play it again?"

After two more screenings, Debbie admitted that Hildy would have to draw a picture, she saw nothing or no one that stood out. All Debbie experienced from the video was a wistful flashback of herself as a teenager, wearing clothes and hairstyles like those onscreen.

Now Hildy doubted her own initial impressions. Surely if this was the man her mother had been married to for twenty-nine years, Debbie would recognize him, whether on sight or by some kind of intuitive connection thing. Could be Hildy had wasted all that time editing images of a stranger, but she wouldn't let it go just yet.

She cued the footage up again, pausing when her dad's face was the clearest. She pointed him out – there behind the face-painted girl – and watched as her mother adjusted her reading glasses to focus on a single time-blurred face out of several in the shot.

"Oh! Oh! Is that David? Is that your dad?" Debbie's hands flew to her mouth and her eyes moistened with sentiment.

Hildy misted over in empathy and said quietly, almost reverently, "Well, you'd be the expert on that."

Debbie touched her husband's young face on the screen with her finger, the wedding ring digit. Hildy felt as if she vanished from the room and all that remained were her parents, electronically reunited after seven years. The air in the room softened and filled with reminiscence. The daughter allowed the widowed mother a soundless moment to go wherever these pictures had taken her.

After Debbie had viewed the clips three more times, she shook herself back to the present and listened to Hildy's tale of how this had come to be.

Debbie said, "I never knew he'd attended Monterey Pop. You know I didn't meet him until late '69 when we worked together at the restaurant. He was my daddy's worst nightmare — a twenty-one year old Vietnam vet dating his sheltered seventeen-year-old daddy's girl. I remember that David was very into music for the first two or three months we dated – unusually so. He could pull song lyrics and band names out of his head like a regular encyclopedia. If I'd met him today, I could nickname him Google." Her whole face smiled.

"Ma, you look seventeen right now," Hildy said with her face propped in her hand like a child enthralled. "So, he never talked about being in San Francisco in sixty-seven?"

"I'm sorry, Hil, I don't recall him saying anything at all about living in or visiting San Francisco that year. Probably because he was drafted that fall, only a couple of months after that concert, and we know his war experience changed everything. He'd only been back from Vietnam for three months when we met. And even if he did mention the Monterey Pop Festival, it may not have meant anything to me, a Southern girl who loved the Beatles and Sam the Sham and the Pharaohs, sure, but I knew more about beloved authors than favorite bands. Monterey Pop was not as legendary, not as romanticized as Woodstock. Besides, the late sixties were so full of cultural events that this one was merely part of the mélange."

"Wow, I wish I could talk to Daddy right now," Hildy said reflectively. "For lots of reasons, but now I'm so curious about his early life. I guess I was always okay with knowing so little because of the ... you know, his ongoing issues. But now, to stumble across a piece of his history and have no way to fill in the blanks ...."

"My daughter, the reporter," Debbie said with a smile. "I can't help you with details of your dad's life in 1967. He was a lot of fun when I met him in '69 but I could see, or maybe sense, the serious undertones. And of course, within the next several years, the dark side came to dominate. I believe his pain and the tragic memories changed his life. But, you should never doubt that he was a really good guy."

Debbie told her daughter that she wanted some time to think back over the history, maybe look again at her photo albums. They'd talk again after that.

***

By the time he was unintentionally archived on film at the Monterey Pop Festival, David Fallon, an only child, had already been orphaned and taken in by his grandparents until he finished high school. He told the young Debbie that to deal with his loss he'd thrown himself into his high school studies and his new love — music — before deciding to forgo college. His fervor to be a guitar-playing rock star matched the dreams of many of his peers. He worked odd jobs and fast food which earned him not only a meager, bohemian living, but also a draft ticket to the conflict in Southern Asia. The frustrated musician spent eleven and a half months in Vietnam involved in covert operations that would, ironically, sour him on the very music he'd once immersed himself in as a means of sustaining his grief-edged sanity.

Eventually, the songs and bands he had once revered and emulated became a soundtrack to his wakeful nightmare in

Vietnam. The spit-in-his-face non-welcome-back he received when he returned home, coupled with a naïve assumption that life was as he'd left it, sent him reeling from the decisions and difficulties of a life that he'd never planned for.

He saw in Debbie a possibility for some scrap of normalcy. Initially suppressing any desire to confess his demons, he was convinced that sharing his inner blackness would likely send her running away from him and his complex issues to search out someone more like herself. But the teenage girl proved a sympathetic listener and friend and eventually much more. David came to believe that she was his own personal second chance at a life and a family. If she wouldn't have him, well, he couldn't see a happy alternative.

Debbie thought about all these things, the few secret, deep places that her beloved but troubled husband had entrusted to her. She concluded that it had to be okay to keep *some* things between husband and wife, to exclude even a daughter, no matter how curious. Hildy had grown up a witness to her father's fragile constitution, but was only given a basic, general explanation. David had taken most of his secrets to his grave, and most of those that he'd shared with Debbie would go with her to her own.

***

The interest in classic rock music that had been nourished in Hildy as she watched the footage of the Monterey Pop Festival took deeper root. The information available to her from the internet and the reference material in the studio's archives fed her hunger for facts and background. She learned more from her mother about the sounds of the revolution, how it felt to be present when this music was in its rowdy toddler stage. The tidbits about David Fallon's early passion for music that slipped into these conversations served to flesh out Hildy's rather one-dimensional memories of her father. In this new infatuation with vintage rock and roll, she felt an affectionate bond with her dad that she'd never known, even before he died. A bittersweet awareness, as it also brought regret at having missed this opportunity while her father lived.

Debbie insisted, when she and her daughter had these conversations, that Hildy lamented a non-existent missed chance. Debbie explained repeatedly that the war had effectively severed David's single-minded early drive toward music and that he'd certainly not have been amenable to sharing this interest with his daughter. She felt it very well could have pushed him deeper into the dark world that defined his post-war life.

Hildy loved her mother and was growing to deeply respect the devotion that she carried for her damaged husband, how difficult their personal relationship must have truly been.

But she disagreed wholeheartedly with her mother's insistence on this issue. To Hildy, there was every chance that nurturing this common interest could have made a positive difference in her father's mental health. But this grand experiment in hindsight could never be proved or refuted.

***

A few days later in a staff meeting at work, Hildy was inspired by some of the free-flowing ideas about upcoming projects at the TV station. She sought out her team leader and said that she wanted to run some thoughts by her. Aileen suggested that they get together later that day but Hildy asked for a couple of days to arrange her material in a tighter format. Aileen seemed impressed with the cryptic proposal and told Hildy she looked forward to the unveiling.

The sore neck muscles that habitually resulted from Hildy's job were nothing compared to what ensued after twenty hours in high editing gear. First, she hashed out some issues with her mother and, surprised and pleased with the results, set about to tell one man's story. A sensitive touch with the personal aspects of her father's life coalesced with the recorded material Hildy had put together, merging into the outline of her project. She now had something solid to show her boss.

***

Hildy's documentary was scheduled to air two weeks later on a Tuesday evening in the half-hour segment available to local programming that followed the 6:00 news. Aileen had been sold by Hildy's comment that many of David Fallon's contemporaries would surely relate to the story's subject matter. Aileen had pressed for an earlier air date, to more directly benefit from the tie-in that Hooch Conrad had unwittingly provided. But Hildy begged for adequate editing time, not willing to sacrifice quality and accuracy for expediency.

Hildy and Debbie were together for the premiere, but they'd already seen the finished product several times. They declined the invitations from close friends to have a watch party, preferring a private viewing. Mother and daughter wanted to share the public maiden voyage of this very personal project exclusively with each other.

***

As she watched, Debbie naturally related to the deeply personal aspects of the project, but Hildy had taken painstaking care to protect her father's most private challenges, those that were strictly not for public consumption. Not only was there no hint of exploitation, the talented daughter had created a positive, loving tribute to the father she quite possibly knew better now than ever before. Debbie delighted in the musical aspects of the piece. After all, they were a large part of her history as well.

The final credits rolled and mother and daughter clapped and whooped at each mention of Hildy Fallon's name. They fell into each other's arms in an emotional heap, weeping until the phones started ringing. They spoke to congratulatory friends and family until they each had to beg for mercy, pleading the lateness of the hour.

Both women slept the sleep that comes with relief and release.

***

Hildy arrived at the TV station the next morning to accept applause and accolades both sincere and campy. A full voice-mail box and forty-seven new emails would take her the better part of the morning to wade through. Most of the messages were from friends or colleagues and ran the gamut from formal and congratulatory to silly. She was addressed as Ms. Memoir and Rocumentary Queen. One message from a former college roommate asked her what she planned to wear to collect her Emmy.

But the most noteworthy, serendipitous communication of all had been forwarded to her from the station's general email address. It read:

Thank you so much for the very moving documentary, Monterey Papa.

*I thought you may be interested to know that I also appeared in the concert audience sitting near David Fallon. That's me with the **I LUV YOU** on my face. I didn't know David, but after watching your glowing tribute to him, I wish I had.*

Thank you again for a well-done, interesting program and my husband and I hope you give us more of the same.

Mary Harmseth Dulles (a.k.a. "Harmony" back in the day) ha.

Debbie Fowler

Debbie Fowler was born in the middle of the legendary Baby Boom and has always been fascinated by the fascination with this demographic. She has raised a family and worn many hats during her many decades. She enjoys writing about The Most Famous Generation and is the author of an upbeat, nostalgia-sprinkled novel: *'62 Chevy, an Auto-Biography*, the imagined story of consecutive owners of a 1962 Impala over the course of 45 years. Buy it on Amazon.

Debbie and her husband Wayne live in Arkansas and are the authors of the blog *easilyamusedroadrunners.com* where they write about their frequent road trips or various and sundry topics they find entertaining or interesting.

WHISTLE IN THE FOG
BY GERALDINE HAWLEY

419 PC Henry Marshall drew his cape about him and paused in the shelter of a shop doorway for an illicit smoke. As he did so, Big Ben struck the hour. Idly he counted the strokes. Thirteen! He must have counted one stroke twice; sounds were deceptive in fog like this. He finished the cigarette and continued on his beat up Regent Street towards Piccadilly.

It was a dank, miserable night in November. The fog had crept up from the river and visibility was about ten yards. The street lights were like little golden pools, lighting only their immediate vicinity, before being pushed back on themselves by the denseness of the fog. Few people were about at this hour.

Henry paused again and shined his torch into the doorway of a large department store. It was very dark. A time switch turned off the lights at midnight. A flicker of movement caught the corner of his eye. He turned, just in time to see a figure sliding past his shoulder. A girl. Dressed in something long and flowing and quite unsuitable for such a night. He shrugged; she'd looked a shapely bird but the cold and the fog dampened his enthusiasm for a second glance. He turned his torch back to the windows. Bit bare, he thought, not usual for 'em to have no models on display.

The fog was thicker now. Henry stopped for a moment to check his bearings. It was then that he saw them: four tall, elegant figures walking out of a plate glass window! He was so near he could have touched their painted faces. They glided swiftly and purposefully past him and were lost in the murky night. As they disappeared he heard the faint echo of a thin, sibilant voice. "We must hurry. The leader waits at..."

Henry was a very young policeman and this was his first spell of night duty. He felt inside his tunic for his radio, reassured by its solid weight. As he plodded on, shining his torch into the shops, he noted again that none of them contained any display models. It was difficult to see what was real and what was imagination, but the pavement seemed full of silent figures, gliding past like wraiths. He leaned against a doorway and turned, his eyes darting left and right to try and make out what was happening. Sometimes the figures would come into focus but then, when he blinked, there was nothing but fog.

It was a filthy night. The damp seemed to go right through his cape and uniform into his very bones. He shuddered. Out of the fog loomed a tall figure in a flowing cloak and Henry made up his mind to follow. He moved as silently as possible and felt that as he melted away from the street lights and into the fog, he might be mistaken for one of them himself.

Other figures kept appearing and he found himself almost rubbing shoulders with mandarins, milkmaids, male and female figures in every sort of costume from evening dress to underwear, uniform and ski clothes. He caught quick glimpses as they passed beneath the street lights. Their faces looked neither right nor left and shocked him with their fixed, painted eyes. They were expressionless, all intent on getting...wherever it was they were going.

Henry had long since lost his bearings when he saw a light glimmering ahead, which proved to be a sign for an underground station. Good, he thought, with relief, now I can find out where I am. But the letters were all jumbled up, ERERPAGNK, and made no sense. He was completely hemmed in by figures, with no choice but to go down the steps.

Down and down they went, taking the fog with them, until finally they stopped and Henry walked on into a darkness faintly illuminated by weir lights, which glowed like green coals suspended in the air. He wondered nervously what he was getting himself into. This lot wasn't a football crowd. Those, he has been trained to cope with (although not alone) and anyway, he couldn't use his radio so far underground. It was too late to turn back; he was being hurried along by the silent figures behind him. He curled his clammy fingers inside his gloves to try and stop them shaking. It was eerie, like a spooky film. He told himself that it might be a bizarre fancy dress party but his better judgement knew that this wouldn't account for the participants walking through shop windows, nor for that matter would it explain why some of them were so scantily clad yet oblivious to the cold.

Ahead of them now was a flashing green light and they entered what appeared to be a vast vaulted chamber. The green atmosphere was softened by a misty vapour and Henry found it difficult to see how large the place was or how many of the phantom figures were gathered together. As far as he could see the place was crowded with them, all gazing straight ahead. He strained his eyes to see what they were looking at so intently.

As he focused on the farthest part of the chamber, a bigger cloud of green arose and, beneath it, he glimpsed what appeared to be an enormous glass bowl. In the centre of the bowl was a heaving mass of green fluorescence, emitting hundreds of sparks into the air, which then turned into the green vapour. The mist was getting so thick that it completely engulfed the bowl.

In a few seconds the green mist turned a darker green, then black, and then there was a bubbling noise from inside the bowl. A strange yellowish light shone eerily in the middle of the dark shadows where the bowl was now hidden.

The figures on either side of Henry joined their palms together in front of their chests and inclined their heads, remaining in this position. Henry hastily did the same and, looking sideways, discovered that he was between a girl in a long blue dress and a man in ski clothes. The silence was broken by a soft voice which hissed gently as it spoke but could be heard quite clearly.

"My children," it said. "We are gathered here tonight to strike for our freedom and wreak havoc on the earth animals. We Zircoids have waited thousands of years for this opportunity and tonight we shall see the destruction of those soft-fleshed earth humans who know so little compared with our civilization. We have been patient, but we need be patient no longer. Our time has come. Since our planet Zirca has been conquered we shall take over this backward earth and once more be the rulers of our own destiny."

The voice stopped and there was a sound like autumn leaves rustling. Henry looked at his companions, who were rubbing their fingertips together in silent applause. He did the same.

The voice went on to give in detail the plans for the complete destruction of the human race. A plan so diabolical that Henry barely kept himself from exclaiming in horror. He raised his head slightly and looked round to see if anyone had noticed. Not one of the shadowy figures had stirred. They stood with joined palms and bent heads, their painted eyes gazing at the floor.

The voice continued. "I shall control events from the Brain of Zirc, our Leader, who has awakened after centuries, and given us this plan which surely cannot fail. Zirc is here, with us, but in other places there are millions more like you, my friends. To them Zirc is speaking through other channels."

The voice became louder now, hissing and full of menace. "Remember that when you leave here Zirc will be in control of your minds and actions, and when you do as he directs be confident that we shall triumph and Zirca will rise again on earth." The voice dropped again and became fainter. "When all is over the Brain of our leader will sleep again, to be ready when we need him."

The voice died away and for an instant the yellow light flared to show the smoky glass bowl and its contents. The light gradually faded and there was nothing left but a grey mist, as if the fog had somehow found its way into the underground chamber. At the far end there was a green glow that began to get brighter and the vapour turned to green again. The lights by the entrance began to glow and the listeners bowed, turned around and began to glide silently away. Henry found himself once more caught up in the moving throng.

His one idea was to get out and use his radio to call the station, but as he tried to elbow his way to the front, forgetting for the moment that he was in danger himself, the two figures nearest to him turned. They could only see when facing front as their painted eyes could not move, and as Henry pushed to extricate himself from the crowd they followed him.

"This is not one of us," the one in ski clothes hissed. It stretched out a hand and a hard, cold finger touched Henry's cheek. "See – he is warm and soft. We must dispose of him."

Henry flung up his arm to protect his eyes as the spiky fingers poked at his face and other hands pushed him. He grabbed an arm and twisted it. To his horror it came away in his hand. He brandished it in front of him to try and ward off the others, but more of them, attracted by the scuffle, were closing in on him and kicking him with their hard plaster feet and digging their sharp fingers into various parts of his body. He flailed about with the arm and hit one of them, then the arm broke in half and dropped to the ground where it shattered into little pieces.

Henry took one hand from his face to feel for his truncheon but was knocked to his knees. His groping hand felt his whistle through his tunic pocket, securely fastened on its chain. Not thinking what he was doing, he drew it out before he was pushed flat on the floor to be brutally kicked again. None of the self-defence tactics he had learned was of any use against these fleshless figures who felt nothing, just stared at him with their unmoving eyes while they stabbed and kicked.

In desperation he rolled and twisted to try and evade the blows, one hand over his eyes and the other still clutching his whistle. It was hopeless, of course, to expect help to come in a place like this, but it was all he had, and the noise might at least make them pause for a moment and give him a chance.

He struggled to get the whistle to his lips. When he eventually succeeded, his mouth was too dry and nothing happened when he blew. With his face scarlet from exertion and a creeping numbness spreading through his body, he mustered all his breath and what little strength he had left and eventually managed a faint "peep".

The feet and fingers paused. With renewed effort he blew again, an ear-splitting blast that echoed around the underground chamber.

For a few seconds there was silence. Then from the far side of the chamber came a faint, low moan that stopped suddenly on a choking gurgle. All at once great numbers of sparks flew up and foul black smoke rose in the air. The plaster dummies faltered and swayed. They looked as if they were engaged in a grotesque slow dance, turning aimlessly this way and that.

Henry staggered to his feet, coughing and choking, and stumbled out into the passage. It was completely dark. The green lights that had lighted the way in were gone. He felt in his pocket for his torch and was surprised to find it still there. The glass was cracked but when he switched it on its beam shone out and he slowly and painfully made his way to the steps.

He was almost there when a tremendous blast shook the ground underneath him and he was thrown off his feet to land at the foot of the stairs. The torch flew out of his hand and rolled away. Miraculously the bulb stayed intact and the torch lay there, shining up the steps and outlining the crumpled body in dark blue at the bottom.

Henry opened his eyes to find himself propped against a wall. One of his colleagues was rubbing his hands and another was putting his radio back in his pocket. Henry felt his head and blinked. It was daylight. Last night's fog had gone, leaving just a light mist and drizzle.

The constable grinned at Henry.

"Thought you were a goner," he said cheerfully. "George and I have been looking for you ever since you didn't report at 2am. Thought you'd fallen down a drain in the fog!"

Henry was silent as the events of the night came back to him. It was much too far-fetched to try to explain. He looked about him and saw that he was by the subway to Green Park station.

The two constables hauled him to his feet. George dusted him down and then looked about him. "Can't see your helmet anywhere," he said, "it's probably been pinched for a souvenir by a passing drunk!"

"Better take you back to the station," the other constable said. "You look as if you've been taking on the army by yourself. Sarge's been like an anxious father. What happened?" he added, as between them they helped Henry over to a police car parked around the corner. Henry remained silent. His head ached and his body felt bruised all over. He leaned back and shut his eyes.

George drove gently along the deserted streets to the station. When they arrived, the constables helped Henry into the breakroom and settled him in an armchair.

"You stay with him," said George. "I'll go and find the Sergeant and a nice cup of tea."

Henry relaxed and shut his eyes again. Even then he could still see the painted faces and terrible eyes as they poked and kicked him. He shuddered. George returned with the tea, and while he was drinking it the Sergeant came in.

"What happened to you, Henry?" he asked. "Fell down the steps in the dark, did you? It was a real pea souper, filthy night. Hardly even fit for coppers to be out."

The police surgeon appeared, looking not very pleased to have been dragged out of bed. He gave Henry a swift examination.

"I think you'll live," he said briefly. "Ribs bruised, cuts and abrasions but mostly shock. Twenty-four hours in bed, and you'll be as good as new." He scribbled out a note and gave it to George. "Casualty at St Thomas's should sort him out. Treat him gently." He snapped his bag shut and turned to go.

"Odd thing." He paused with his hand on the door handle. "Drove past the Houses of Parliament on my way here and the clock's stopped. Still says 1am. Never known Big Ben to stop except when he's being serviced or repaired, and then it's well publicized."

So it wasn't a nightmare, thought Henry. Now I have to write a report. Will anybody believe me and do I believe it myself? They think I slipped down the steps in the fog. Better leave it like that. The whistle must have shattered the radio waves controlling the Zircoids or something.

He closed his eyes again but the painted faces swayed in front of him and his bruised and battered body ached. The Sergeant looked at him closely. "Well, get a move on," he said to the two constables. "Get an ambulance and get him to St Thomas's and one of you stay with him. I want to know what happened."

One constable and the Sergeant left the room, closing the door gently behind them. George tucked a blanket round Henry and sat down with his back to him, drawing out his notebook to write his report.

Henry opened his eyes. He couldn't see the figures any more, only the comforting sight of George's back. He felt in his pocket for his whistle. It was still there. He carefully pulled it out and for a moment his heart missed a beat. Jammed in one of the links of the chain was what looked like a human finger! He pushed the whistle back into his pocket. His own report could wait. All he wanted was to sleep and forget his aching body and the sinister models. There'd be time enough tomorrow!

Geraldine Hawley

Gerry Hawley is an ex-Wren, Royal Marine wife and mother of three, granny of five. In 25 years she moved house 29 times, twice overseas. She has written short stories and poems for years and done a good deal of writing of pantomime scripts for the local amateur dramatic club. She started her parish magazine and went on to edit it for nine years. Recently widowed after 64 years, she shares a cottage on a Somerset village green with a small, elderly and eccentric Springer Spaniel.

The One That Got Away
By Ernesto Marcos

"Here, on this once secluded beach is where I first met her," he said to the bartender, delighted to have an audience, even if it was an audience of only one. An hour earlier, the seventy-plus-year-old man had ridden on a bicycle rented from the Ritz-Carlton in Key Biscayne past the gatehouse of Bill Baggs Cape Florida State Park. It was still early enough that some of the rattan barstools remained on the countertop.

The old man had the bartender's complete, if unenthusiastic, attention. "So, so adventurous and gentle she was. What you might call a free spirit, uninhibited. Respected folks, you know, but never cared what they thought of her." His eyes lit up. "A kinder, sweeter soul you'll never meet." He polished off his second Dos Equis. They served as chasers for the two miniature bottles of Scotch he brought with him, just in case the outdoor bar happened not to sell hard liquor—turned out he made a good call. He used the beer bottle to point at stretches of ridging sand dunes, a scatter of sea grapes and pines. "Nothing here then—'cept for that old lighthouse over there.

"Another, sir?"

The old man looked at his watch. It had stopped working almost as soon as he left the hotel. Didn't matter. Time was of no consequence today.

"What's your name, son? Mine's Charlie, Charlie T. Conner, Jr." He offered his hand.

"Manny." The bartender reciprocated.

"It couldn't be a lovelier day could it, Manny?"

"No, sir. We wouldn't have it any other way. Another beer, Mr. Connor?"

"No, no thanks. I want to get some fishing in while I can still walk." Mr. Connor showed Manny his handy-dandy fishing rod. The bartender turned to answer the telephone. "You say the fishing area's beyond the pine trees?" Manny nodded. "Can I leave my bike there?" A stiff wind ruffled the old man's hair. At least he still had some—gray but full.

The barman covered the receiver with his hand. "Yessir, that's right." He pointed toward a copse of trees. "Over there. Your bike's cool where you left it."

"Restroom?"

"Inside the restaurant first right." Charlie pushed past the entrance door, veered right and made a quick pit stop. Beer has a way of forcing the issue, he concluded.

***

"There were no gatehouses fifty years ago," Charlie said, crossing the picnic area toward the beach, "or paved roads or parking lots or… Manny. Heck, the place didn't even have an official name in those days. Locals dubbed it Lighthouse Beach."

As he neared the designated fishing area, a young woman, in a dark blue bikini splashed out of the ocean and ran dripping to a waiting beach blanket spread flat on the sand. She removed a towel from a huge bag, dried her pinkish skin, and wrapped it around her head. For some peculiar reason, the woman's movements disconcerted Charlie—the way her body, long arms and legs moved fluidly, carefree. Vaguely familiar somehow. He decided she probably wasn't from these parts. A tourist. Undoubtedly attractive. Don't be an old fool, Charlie. Shaking his head, he walked on.

Charlie found shade under a spindly coconut palm and cast a line over the breakers. He reeled it in a bit screwed a hole several inches deep into the ground using the bottom of his fishing pole and braced it with rocks. Twisting his butt into the sand, he leaned back into the palm. Brief moments later, the old man kicked off his shoes and then peeled off his socks, sliding his feet under the coarse sand. The waves rolled in sounding like intimate applause. Nothing else interrupted the silence. Charlie opened his mouth and gobbled up puffs of air.

As of yet, he hadn't decided what to do with the fish he would catch. "Can't hardly cook 'em inside the hotel room. Maybe the hotel keeps a barbecue grill on the grounds for guests. You haven't caught any yet, Charlie ol'boy. Let's cross that bridge when we get to it."

The gentle breeze, the saltwater smell even the echoing squawks of seabirds made him drowsy. The sun warmed his uncovered head and softened his eyelids. Just as he was about to doze off, a tall young man, dark tanned skin contrasting with sun-bleached hair and similar in age to the girl in the blue bikini strode past him heading her direction. Charlie watched the two chat a bit before the guy settled for a halfhearted "see ya" wave and ambled off. "Better luck next time, buddy," whispered the old man through the side of his mouth.

From out of nowhere, for a second—a millisecond—the girl turned her head Charlie's way and smiled. His heart leaped and froze, leaving him not knowing how to respond. By the time he managed a comeback smile, the girl had turned while unwrapping the towel over her head and pulled out a book from inside the big bag. He hoped she would glance back but knew she wouldn't. Only happenstance, old man. Charlie suddenly figured out what had earlier startled him about the girl. It was the way she moved—her gait—her demeanor. No, no, not imagination. Not the sun, the beers, whiskey, or faulty memories of days gone by but a familiar picture of...

I should speak with her, he thought. Nah, the girl's going to think I'm some kind of a kook. His rod wiggled. Charlie grabbed the short pole and felt a slight tension, but it was only a nibble. He reeled the line in then let it fly almost twice the distance as before. After sticking the end of the pole back into the hole, he got up and went to say hello.

***

"Good day, miss. I hope I'm not intruding. I was sitting over there under the tree…" The girl looked up from her book and brought a hand to her eyes but didn't say a word. "Well, you see, you look awfully similar to a person I met here quite a while ago. You remind me of her. I don't want you to think I have an ulterior motive," he said spotting the man she had spoken with beforehand now farther up the beach in conversation with another pretty face. The woman followed Charlie's eyes and smirked.

"Figures," she replied.

"I just don't want you to think I'm one of them fellas."

"Oh, you mean you're not actually hitting on me? Or wanting to be my sweet big ol' sugar daddy?" The girl watched the old man's shoulders sag and face redden. She immediately felt terrible like she'd smacked a puppy or worse.

"N-n-n-no, miss. Ah-ah, I—" Crestfallen, he did an about-face.

"Oh, I apologize," she said genuinely upset. "I'm so sorry. Please don't go." She sprang up and grasped his forearm. "Please, I'm sorry, Mr...."

He stared at the hand holding him in place. Smooth, no spots or wrinkles. "I'm Charlie T. Connor, Jr." He shifted her grip and shook her hand.

"You know, you too kind of remind me of someone I knew when I was younger, Mr. Connor. He may have been about your age then. Big bushy eyebrows and mustache included." Charlie stroked his chin.

"Dr. Furlani my first music teacher."

"You're a musician?"

"Oboist, to be specific. I drove down to Miami for an audition. The New World Symphony has an open seat."

"Good for you. Well…" he said feebly, "well, good luck to you." Charlie turned to leave.

"Please, Mr. Connor, stay. I feel bad enough as it is. Don't make me feel worse. Sometimes I can be so flippant and wicked. I forget that there are gentlemen still in this world." She sat again and patted a spot on the blanket. "Please sit, sir. My name is Judy, by the way."

"Nice to meet you, Miss Judy. And please, call me Charlie. This Mr. Connor stuff makes me feel grandfatherly." He stiffened. "You're sure now. Like I told you, I don't want to intrude."

"I'm sure. How about a beer? I pulled out a couple from my friend's fridge just before I left her place. Should still be cold." Judy rummaged through her bag. "Here we go." She passed him a bottle. "Cheers," she said. Twisting off the caps they drank thirstily.

"You've got a lot of gear inside that sack of yours."

"And then some." Judy laughed. A giggly sort of laugh. A nice wide grin. Comparable to those pixiesque gymnasts you see on TV during the Olympics. The way Emily laughed, he noted.

"What are you reading?" Judy handed Charlie the book. "*The Lost Country* by JR Salamanca. Why this is one of my favorite books."

"Really? The friend I'm staying with recommended it. I borrowed hers."

"This is a wonderful novel. You'll love it." He gave the book back. "It's kinda sad, though but a good sad. You know what I mean?"

"Yeah, I like sad. I do sad well." That same giggle once again. They stared out into the ocean sipping away. The

154

rhythmic ebb and flow of the surf placated their initial awkwardness. "Do you live around here?"

Charlie shook his head. "Nope, just visiting. I like this place. It's changed a lot since my younger days, though." His gaze shifted away from the horizon to the mesmerizing pattern of clouds rolling over the blue-green sea.

Judy took a slow deep breath. "So, you were saying I reminded you of someone? Who?"

He glanced her way. "Emily."

"A long lost love? The one that got away?"

"Well..." He grinned. Staring at her felt strange, but he couldn't help himself. Green eyes sparkled and gazed back at him confidently. Didn't seem this girl had a shy bone in her body. Wispy brown strands of hair swirled in and out of her face unperturbed, not as light as Emily's but close.

"The best day of my life," he said. "I was visiting relatives on the Key and wanted to get a little sun maybe fish some. One morning, purely by chance, I headed out here. I had no idea this beach existed. No signs, nothing. Simply followed foot trails toward the ocean until... well, there it was. By chance, Emily showed up with a group of friends more or less at the same time. They set up a net and played volleyball on the sand near me. I couldn't take my eyes off of her. She was so lithe and sleek. Not one wasted motion in her movements… and gorgeous—like you."

Color came to Judy's cheeks. "Aha," she said clearing her throat. "Guess I could use another beer right about now."

"Oh, I'm sorry. I've made you uncomfortable, haven't I?"

"No, no you're fine. It's just that I have about six hours of practice time staring me in the face and I really have to be on my way."

"Tell you what. Let me buy you a beer before you go. You brought two and gave me one. And now you're thirsty. The least I can do is return the favor."

"No big deal, Charlie. I—"

"Ah, come on. Indulge an old man. You said you could use another beer." He got to his feet. "What do you say? One for the road?"

Judy shrugged her shoulders. "OK, but only one." She pulled out a windbreaker from her bag slipped her arms through its sleeves, scooted up and wriggled into a pair of jean shorts. "Isn't that your stuff over there?" she said, pointing to his fishing rod under the palm tree.

"Oh, they'll be fine. I'll come back for them later."

Once they neared the restaurant, Judy sat at a picnic table located under a thick canopy of trees shading an ivied trellis.

Charlie hopped up a few steps, sidled up to the counter and ordered the beers. He felt spookily lightheaded but chucked it to the warm weather, and the giddiness of nostalgia.

He returned a bit breathless, "Back with two cold ones." They took long greedy pulls almost finishing their beers in one chug. "Ahh, let's see now where was I?"

"On the beach watching the gorgeous Emily kick up the sand with her gorgeous friends."

"But I had eyes only for Emily." Charlie winked. "After the ball rolled over my way several times, they asked if I wanted to join them. Actually, Emily asked. We played until about noon, then the two of us paired off and ran into the ocean for a swim." The old man's eyes trailed off. "We hit it off right away. When Emily and I came out of the water, she took my hand—the way you did earlier—"

"I—"

"And we walked alone on the beach for hours." Charlie blinked out of his reverie. "Yes, yes, I know," he said nodding, "you were trying to be kind. Your hand… So like Emily's—youthful and caressing." Judy guzzled her last two or three mouthfuls. "That was the first of our many endless walks."

The young woman rummaged inside the tent she called a bag and retrieved her phone. She checked the time. "Listen, Mr.

Conner, I apologize. Your story's awfully sweet, but I have to get going."

"Oh, I see we're back to Mr. Connor. Have I offended you?"

"Charlie," she said firmly, "it's time for me to go."

"But we're having such a wonderful time. Wait, I have a better idea. Why don't I buy us a couple of glasses of champagne and toast appropriately? The way it should be done. A farewell toast. For old time's sake."

"Mr. Connor, there are no old times here. No good old times, no bad old times. No times at all!" Judy got to her feet. "Goodbye."

"Wait, wait. I'll bring a bottle." His arms flew open and held up one finger. "One minute, please." He started toward the bar. Judy tucked her face into her chest, shook her head and blew out a long breath. "I'll be right back. Don't go away," he shouted sprinting up the steps.

"Charlie!" He didn't hear her.

Manny looked at the old man warily as Charlie moved toward him with a wild-eyed grin. "I'll have a bottle of your finest champagne, my good man."

A grin spread across the bartender's face. He rolled his eyes. "It's not that you've had *that* much to drink, but sometimes the hot sun, the—"

"You can't be serious. Trust me, Manny. This is it," he babbled. "The young lady has to leave in a minute, so this is definitely the last one."

"Young lady?"

"Yes, Emily—I mean Judy—we met on the beach. She's waiting at one of the picnic tables behind this screen. I'll need two glasses."

"Where are you staying, sir?"

"What? Oh, the Ritz-Carlton, up the road. Why?"

"I'm going to call and have them send a car. There's no way you'll be able to ride that bicycle after a bottle of champagne."

"You're a good man, Manny."

The bartender went to the fridge, brought back the champagne, a couple of glasses and set them on a tray. "Here's your Vieux and two glasses. Best we've got."

"Thank you very much. You're a scholar and an astronaut."

Manny laughed. "OK. But be careful going down those steps." The bartender cringed when Charlie half-tripped, half skipped down the stairs yet somehow recovered his balance and did not drop the tray or topple over.

"There's a reason I didn't stumble." Charlie only mouthed the words. "I'm walking on air!" He laughed loudly.

Precariously, Charlie's feet carried him toward the picnic table where he left Judy. But when he arrived, Judy was gone. Was this the right place? He scanned the area. Yes, this is it. "Judy? Where are you?"

The old man set the tray down. He felt woozy. "Judy?" Maybe she's in the ladies' room, he thought. No, the restrooms are located inside the restaurant. She would have passed me on the way in. "Judy?" Those gathered at other tables turned away trying to ignore him. Charlie staggered left and then right. "Have you seen a young woman?" he asked the few still maintaining eye contact. "Judy? She was just here. We were going to have champagne." He spun in place teetering from side to side. A sudden sadness caused him to shiver. "Judy! Judy!" His legs buckled and he fell hard face-first. People gasped. Two teenage boys ran over and hoisted him up by the elbows.

"Are you alright, mister?"

"Don't worry, guys, I got this." Manny grabbed hold of Charlie propped him up under his arm and carted the old man back to the table. He stepped back a bit assessing Charlie's condition. "You don't look too bad. Are you OK?" Charlie's head bobbed dejectedly. "Now, you need to settle down. I heard the ruckus all the way to the bar. Let's open your bottle of bubbly so you can relax until your car arrives. Not that you need any more of this, but—"

"But what about Judy? She couldn't have just left."

"Look, Mr. Connor for the moment there doesn't seem to be a Judy or anyone else for that matter." He gently patted the old man's shoulder. "Maybe she'll return." Manny popped the cork. The champagne fizzed and rimmed over as the bartender swiftly poured. "There you go. Now take it easy I've got to get back. Your hotel said they'd send a car as soon as possible. Should be only a few minutes."

Charlie brought the glass to his lips and tasted the effervescence. With a sobering glance, he said, "She's not coming back is she, Manny?"

Afternoon shadows encroached like the ticks of a fast clock at journey's end. Charlie scowled at the empty bottle of champagne. He lifted it above his eyes then balanced the bottle on the bridge of his nose filtering a sky of glass—a distorted, imperfect vision of reality. "As through a glass darkly," he mumbled past numb lips. "That was George Patton, wasn't it?" He grabbed the bottle by the neck and tilting his head back, stuck his tongue into the opening. Gently, more or less surreptitiously, the soft crunching sound of tires on gravel drew near. Charlie turned and saw the Ritz-Carlton limo drive up and stop. A uniformed fellow, wearing sunglasses exited the driver's side of the vehicle.

"Mr. Connor?"

"Uh-huh."

"We were called and asked to collect you, sir."

Charlie thought about it for a moment or two. "Hmm, right, Manny, yes. Said he'd request a car. Nice guy Manny. I owe him some money though. I'll be right back."

"That's already been taken care of, Mr. Connor."

"Really? Was he tipped well?" The chauffeur nodded unequivocally. Charlie pointed to the bicycle rack. "The bike's over there."

"Not a problem, sir. I'll go and fetch it," he said and stepped to the rear door holding it open. Charlie managed, without embarrassing himself too much, to make it on his own. A well-dressed, elderly woman sat stiffly on the opposite end of the backseat. The door thumped behind him as he slid on the squeaky leather. Watery green eyes glared at his shoeless feet. A minute or two later the driver returned and started the car.

"Well, looks like you've managed to make a fool out of us once again."

Charlie squeezed his temples and sighed.

"Nice to see you too, Emily." The soundproof glass separating the driver from his passengers activated discreetly. Charlie tried to look out the window past Emily, but her face blocked his line of vision.

"You and your ridiculous fantasies. They never end, do they?" Her eyes narrowed. "What will people think, mmm?"

"I'm sorry, dear. I can't imagine what people will think."

"Don't be smart." Her eyes were drawn once again to Charlie's bare feet. Emily's chin rose pointedly. "A park employee called the hotel and told the front desk attendant you were harassing a woman at the beach like some sort of drunken pervert." The limo U-turned onto the paved road and bounced over a few speed bumps before it proceeded to the exit.

"It wasn't that way at all I—"

"Shut up, Charles."

The car trundled on. A chill, oppressive silence seemed almost to consume the very air he breathed. Charlie wished he had one of those mini whiskey bottles in his pocket. All at once, he perked up and tapped on the glass. "Oh, wait, driver, stop."

The driver lowered the partition a couple of inches. "Sir?"

"There in front of those pine trees up ahead, stop please."

The car slowed and came to a standstill. Charlie didn't wait for the chauffeur to walk around. He opened the door himself and eased out quickly.

"Charles, where are you going?" his wife demanded.

"My fishing rod, Emily. I nearly left it behind." He gazed between the tree trunks, then at Emily. "Look, dear don't you remember this place?"

"Stop being ridiculous, Charles. I've never been here in my life. And neither have you! There's—" The car door slammed shut.

Still a bit woozy, Charlie tottered somewhat in the soft sand but avoided a fall. When he reached the spot where he thought he had left the fishing rod—

"Hey, where is it? Damn, if only… I wonder if somebody ran off with it." He saw his shoes and socks, the dug-up hole alongside the palm tree, the rocks, but no rod. Charlie shuffled about until he noticed a line traced in the sand that stretched from the hole to the water. His pole must have hooked something. "Something big a stingray or horseshoe crab or…" He watched his hands stretch open about two feet, "… or maybe a nice juicy red snapper. That's what it was: a huge snapper." The space between his hands spread further. "I betcha the fish dragged the pole into the ocean. Didn't see that coming. Oh, well, shouldn't have left it unattended," he said, surprisingly stoic.

A dearth of swimmers and sunbathers gave way to a moonscape of abandoned footprints. Shadows fanned in from the west.

"Seems more like the beach of times past," the old man whispered. He tapped his watch and brought it to his ear. "Hmm, darn thing's still stuck." With a grunt Charlie crouched down, settling back against the palm. Warm breezes swept off the ocean and rustled the pines. He swayed slightly, opened his mouth, and gulped down a few select morsels.

Ernesto Marcos

My former employer once posted photographs of employees with thirty years of service. Photos of when they were first hired. I stared at one barely recognizing the woman in the picture, when my boss saw me and said, "Getting old sucks, doesn't it? But it sure beats the alternative." *Not in her case!*

"Getting old sucks" is only a part of the story. Sure I can't beat my grandchildren in a footrace anymore, mirrors are to be avoided at all costs, and I spend more time naked at the doctor's than I do with my wife. But it's not all bad— now my time belongs to *me*. I do the things of *my* choosing, I don't write memos anymore I write whatever my imagination conjures up. I wake up without an alarm clock and drink wine whenever it pleases me. Best of all, I nap comfortably in my bed instead of hiding behind a computer screen. In a nutshell: it's the new story of the old guy. Sure beats the alternative!

An American Story
By Susan McLane

Atlantic Ocean, 1740

Crouched in the darkness of the ship's hold, the passengers await the end of the tempest. Finally the hatch opens, freeing them to seek the fresh air of the deck, where they stretch their storm-tightened muscles. Catarina reaches down for sturdy William and *liebling* Peter as her Peter reaches down for her, smiling into her blue eyes in spite of the sudden weakness that came on him yesterday. Only a week is left before the end of their ocean journey that started in Germany, wended through Amsterdam, and eventually will land them on the soil of Pennsylvania. Soon they will live in a land where they are free to worship as they please.

Later that evening, Peter's fatigue worsens, and he develops a fever. She tends to him as best as she can. The next morning she awakens, expecting her *Guten Morgen* kiss, but the stiffening chill of death has replaced his fever. Distraught, Catarina neglects her crying twins, unable to rise from the cocoon of her sleeping quarters to watch Peter's shrouded body slip over the edge of the ship into the *wasser*.

In light of this calamity, she struggles to formulate a plan. Huddled within a circle of fellow travelers, she learns about the Ephrata Cloister, shelter for her as a widow with Peter and William. She will never be able to marry again because of the vow of chastity required to live in the community, but at least she will not have to worry about their safety. They will be surrounded by brethren speaking the same language and following the same beliefs in this colonial land called America.

Fort Dobbs, North Carolina 1760

Sheltered behind the fort's timbers, soldiers and villagers hear the Indian war whoops and prepare for an attack during the French and Indian War. Blond brothers Peter and William are seasoned by now, well aware of the need to doze with a tomahawk under their pillow. The many escorts they have provided to loyal settlers and Indians alike have honed them to hypervigilance in preparation for attacks. Together they decided on the necessity of this southbound adventure and opportunity to earn money, even if their mother's *auf wiedersens* and oft-sung musical compositions still ricochet across their thoughts in rare moments of calm. At least she is safe in the confines of the Cloister. She took the vow of chastity out of necessity, but it is not for them.

They hunker down beside a newly arrived Scots-Irish teen with fierce green eyes. If ever there was a born warrior, Angus is he. Experience in repelling the Irish off his family's hard-worked Ulster land has scarred Angus' family's skin. But his recent leave-taking because the bloody Brits had exorbitantly increased the rent on the loam they plowed for generations scars his heart. Now he fights for land in a new country—his country—he corrects himself, and imagines the fertile fields he will plant on his own soon-awarded plot, imagines the new generations that will inhabit the soil his calloused hands will tame from virgin forests. The three men ready their muskets while scanning the area leading up to the bulwarks. This time, they feel lucky. After the skirmish is finally over, their careful aim has left many redskins on the ground, but they know that bigger battles lie ahead.

Winnsboro, South Carolina 1763

Peter, William and Angus ready the horses and wagons. They arrive from North Carolina today on land granted in Winnsboro, South Carolina. William has heard of profitable trading in the area. Angus itches to plant crops for the coming season, and Peter's new surveying job awaits.

Orangeburg, South Carolina 1838

Lightfoot carries young Will in a papoose on her back as she stirs their dinner in a black pot over the fire. She preserves some traditional practices even though she stayed behind instead of following the others on the Trail of Tears. William arrived home a few minutes ago with many furs from this moon's trading ventures, the same as his father and grandfather before him. But he says he is going to meet the men in town as soon as they finish supping. He's been gone hunting so long, and now he will leave again straightaway. Why can't he stay in one place for long? She stares at the old scar on his face, the brand he received as punishment for stealing a horse. Should she hide some of the furs he brought home in case he loses his profits in the card games again tonight? What kind of a mood will he be in if he drinks too much of the firewater?

Winnsboro, South Carolina 1850

Colleen's red hair dances around her face as she listens to her husband Peter's story. Something about the way he shares his granda's adventure stories reminds her of the Irish lilt of her uncles' tales, and she rubs her stomach in anticipation of the newest babe she will soon bring into the world. The piecework slips lower on her lap as her mind drifts back to days on the Emerald Isle. But no more, she reminds herself, pulling the cloth up higher and determinedly stitching, dashing away memories of ravaged bodies piled in the streets waiting for burial. The only escape from the potato scourge was flight to America. She has to focus on her remaining family's future here, instead of yearning for lush green hills in the old country. She must gird herself for the sake of this wee one.

Orangeburg, South Carolina 1861

The rhythmic calls and responses of "Wade in the Water" carry across the long rows of cotton as she sways back and forth. Sweat creeps down her back, and her light brown face turns pink during the long hours focused on gathering cotton from the thorny bolls to fill her sack. Massa Angus might not gain as much pleasure from the whip as others she has heard about from slaves who used to toil on the red clay of Georgia, but he still commands a rising profit on the weighing scales, intending to keep the plantation his grandfather started. As well, he has his other demanding ways that can't be argued with. Of course, things could change now that the War just started. She sneaks a hand across her bulging belly covered by rough burlap and wonders whether she will see this child grow up. If it turns out looking one way, she might. If another way, Missus might sell it just like some other slave chillen of a certain look. Some around this area is flapping they lips about freedom being close. She'll believe *that* flight of fancy when she sees it with her own two eyes.

Four years later, the war is over. She heard tell two years ago that her daughter Ruth is only six plantations away, so she directs her bare feet to find her. Finally reaching the end of an avenue of oaks, she discovers from newly freed old timers that her gal has disappeared like a haint.

Lexington, South Carolina 1880

The midwife told Ruth she has to make a decision today. Even though she has succeeded so far in passing, what if the baby comes out dark? Is it worth taking a chance? The risk-taker in her says yes since her gamble has paid off so far. Her cautious side says no since her husband doesn't know she's high yellow. Just then, she feels flickers of butterfly wings inside, and the risk-taker side of her wins.

A few months later, Henry's just-a-little-bit-too-curly head pops out, and her husband lights out for the state line, never to enter South Carolina again.

Lexington, South Carolina 1882

The youngest of Rosa's 13 surviving children has found that pot to bang on again. Their boy wakes up early every morn and always darts back and forth like a tadpole. He can't set still and loves making a racket. The twins burrow in bed beside her, and she can't help but think of the other set that didn't make it a few years back. Will is already out in the fields with the older chirren except Ellen, who has taken to staying home to help her ma with the cooking and young ones since Rosa's sugar is high again. Ellen has shown the most promise in school, and Rosa was hoping she would be able to continue after she won that music award last year, but now the closest Ellen's going to get to the schoolhouse is longingly beholding it out the window. The midwife says Rosa's middle is as swollen this time as it was the last times she popped out her twosomes, and Rosa ponders on the notion that she feels four feet kicking her again. She hopes both babes make it. She and Will need as many hands as possible. Sharecropping don't pay much. Some people asked her when she started going out with Will what kind of white man is a sharecropper, but she didn't pay them no mind since she was love-struck. It's a hard life, but they get by. The worst part is lots of moving. Will always thinks they'll get paid more by another landowner and likes moving from place to place, like his pa did. So far, the sweet-talking that helped him escape the sheriff's wrath when he discovered Will's moonshine hasn't convinced the landowners to give more money for crops though.

 A burnt smell wakes Rosa from her slumber. Then she hears Ellen hollering that her little brother has swallowed the smoke from the fireplace after he got too close and his shirt caught fire. Will comes a'running from the field, then hurls himself in the one-mule wagon to rush the boy to the doc. A few hours later Will returns alone. God musta needed their son real bad because He called him home.

Augusta, Georgia 1893

The wearisome thumping of the looms brings him out of his daydream. Charley, his hair covered with lint, surveys the line of millworkers laboring under the watchful eye of the foreman. At 13, he is one of the youngest scamps working here. His gramps, Angus, is the oldest and sweeps the floors. Gramps couldn't pay the taxes on the plantation after the War, and he lost all his land and tenants. Now it's Charley's honor-bound duty to help provide upkeep for the family, since Papa's injuries in the War won't allow him to work no more. At least Papa's alive, sorta.

Suddenly, the tip of Charley's thumb paints the floor red as it lies squashed under the piece of machinery he couldn't resist touching. Someone binds his thumb. He takes a moment to imagine his mangled digit under the wrapping then gets back to work as the bell that clangs for accidents finally halts. Charley can't afford to miss no time off. He dreams of being a fireman but works in the mill 'til he goes deaf from the clatter of the machines. Later in life, he has the satisfaction of seeing his son Johnny fight fires.

Batesburg, South Carolina 1929

After getting ready for high school, Nina, the latest in at least four generations of red-haired women, strides confidently out of the farmhouse, her homemade dress looking more stylish than the store-bought one her friend sometimes wears. Sewing talent seems to run in their family, plus she can calculate numbers with no trouble a'tall. One day she even came up with the idee of using the *pi* formula to cut out fabric circles for her first quilt. Graduation is almost here, and directly she has to finish sewing her gloves and preparing her salutatory speech. She will try one more time to convince Papa to let her accept the full scholarship to college. Maybe the third time will be the charm. But he doesn't cotton to the idea of allowing girls to attend college.

Nina reluctantly has to turn down the scholarship. Papa is stubborn to change. But God has a plan. A job at the telephone company will have to do. She can also make some pocket change playing the piano at church every Sunday. Years later, somebody hears her playing and singing in church and makes a record for her. Her son Roy loved to listen to it until one day it puzzlingly showed up broken in half. That was after her womb got infected and the doctor whipped it right out and zapped her with radiation. It was also after her firefighter husband Johnny started seeing visions of the baby girl he tried but failed to save.

Aiken County, South Carolina 1951

As Henry fixes the hole in the leaky roof, he thinks over the many other patches this rickety house outside of town needs. He was damn lucky to buy it for his wife and the youngins and his grandmother Ellen through a relaxed federal loan for workers constructing the new Savannah River Plant. America will beat the Commies at their Cold War nuclear game. The good ole U.S. of A. is 'bout to heat things up for them Reds. Let's see how they like that. Houses to rent or buy are near impossible to come by because of so many people pouring into town due to the bomb plant. This house will have to do. He must carve out time to patch up their place, even with all his mandatory overtime, because his daughter Carol is about to become a big sister again. She sings "little ones to him belong..." as she places her hand on her mother's belly and feels her next brother or sister kick in preparation for its approaching arrival. She has helped with the younger brothers and sisters before. Henry tries to focus on hammering and happy sounds like his daughter's singing because they banish memories of his buddies in shark-infested waters during World War II battles.

Aiken, South Carolina 1960

Roy paces in the waiting room, cigars in hand. He didn't know whether to buy pink ones or blue ones, so he got some of both. Shortly afterward, in her hospital room, Carol looks down in shock at one arm covered in a sea of pink and the other in blue. Later, she brushes back a tiny blondish-red lock of Nina Ellen's curly hair, while Roy cautiously traces Peter Lightfoot's straight black tufts. Once they arrive home, the radio starts playing a catchy song, and the twins immediately open their sets of bluish green and brown eyes and gaze around at the menagerie of parents, grandparents, and a couple of great-grandparents ready to enfold them in the arms of family.

Susan McLane

Susan McLane has taught first-year and advanced composition courses at various colleges/universities in North and South Carolina for 25 years. Upon becoming an empty nester in 2017, she decided to investigate creative writing. After attending a few writing workshops, she joined a weeklong writing retreat in the NC mountains, where mention of a nearby bear-sighting a couple of years earlier kept her city-girl feet indoors and her mind exploring. She discovered the words "behavioral epigenetics," which spawned the idea for her first short story. This theory embraces the notion that our genes have deep memory and call out to our current selves whether we know it or not. Discovering through DNA testing that she's 45% German and 25% Scots-Irish reinforced McLane's intuition that her senses awaken when she hears certain traditional German and soaring Scottish music. She likes to imagine her diverse ancestors interacting as they travelled south on the Great Philadelphia Wagon Road in the 1700s. In addition to this short story, McLane had an article published earlier this year analyzing an Emily Dickinson poem. She looks forward to learning and writing more. Whether at the beach or the mountains, she appreciates being able to call the Carolinas home.

Spying on the Gestapo
By Robert L. Nelis

Rita is my part time coworker at the central information desk of a prestigious book store in our city. She is working on a master's in social work. Because my background is so completely differs from hers, she often asks about it. The generation of this interest came about when, by mistake, I told her that during the Second World War my ability to speak French lead to a spy assignment in a Gestapo office. She's forty years younger than me and finds that nasty war to be fascinating. I told her, at two lunches and one dinner, that the story was not interesting, but she continued to ask probing questions.

"Come on Juliette, that sounds exciting and certainly something I will never experience."

My work was secret, but she didn't buy the fact that something from the 1940's could still be under covert restrictions. Her point seemed logical, so I invited her to dinner where I would tell my story. After ordering wine and food I began.

It started, as most things in life, with my mother. Pauline Poulet, a periodic Broadway actress, who usually preformed in smaller venues located around the States. Life, for her, resembled a never-ending performance of a French prima donna character. My birth unfortunately proved to be a major career disruption.

My sister was born eight years before me. At the time of her birth my mother's career, managed by my father, had just taken off. She molded Aimlee into another stage center personality. I came along at the zenith of mother's professional life and required a five-month interruption. While Aimlee continued to be pampered and groomed, my mother dumped me on a series of nannies and baby sitters.

My mother did insist that I learn to speak French. "Juliette, these Americans love all things French, so take advantage." Otherwise, she placed me in a public school in whatever town her show ran.

Reading books became my escape. I remained an indifferent student but would read everything I could put my hands on. Children, when unhappy with their parents, resist the things they force on them. My inferior French caused my mother to often say, "Juliette, you speak like a peasant." She kept after me by speaking to me in the language at least fifty percent of the time. Being a true book-worm dissuaded other students from becoming friends. I managed to finish all formal education without ever having one.

The wave of my mother's vocation finally hit the breakwater when the German army overran France. Within weeks the American love affair with anything French ended. A Chicago theater owner replaced my mother with an understudy. My family's income was eliminated.

It proved impossible to live with my family as we adjusted to the complete collapse of our social position and income stream. Both parents began to abuse alcohol. I chose to take a room in the YWCA and supported myself on a meager salary as a clerk in a parachute manufacturing company. Chicago's central library stood only two blocks from my new abode and it nourished my love of books. Chicago also provided access to a beautiful lake front where I walked and read.

Because of my company's war related work, the federal government sent a variety of employment notices. One notice advertised a job opening for people who could speak French. It paid almost ten times my salary, so I applied

Several weeks later a man arrived at work. Using only French, he interviewed me. Twenty days later, my boss handed me an envelope from Washington DC's Office of Foreign Studies. It contained train tickets and housing vouchers. The letter also ordered my company to give me the necessary time off.

Twenty recruits started meeting in a small Navy Yard brick building. Instructors evaluated our language abilities and we studied the problems the French people faced under Nazi and Vichy governments. My fellow recruits intimidated me. One wrote French poetry, several taught the language at the university level, and some recently lived in the country.

To adjust, I spent my first weekend reading a French history book and taking walks along the Potomac River. I also purchased several magazines containing articles describing Europe's current political situation. Officials ordered us not to socialize with each other nor tell anyone anything about our duties.

On Monday morning of the second week, only half the original class entered the room. An Army officer stood next to the instructor. "I am Colonel Rodger Friday and it is my job to find people who are willing to assist in defeating this horrible enemy. These jobs are interesting and will be critical to the war effort. But before I continue, I must tell you that from this moment forward no one can repeat anything you learn here. *I said never, do you understand?*"

He walked in front of each of us and made a hard evaluation of our faces. Mine registered curiosity.

One of the men from the back asked, "Is this some secret work?"

Friday with a very firm voice said, "Yes, and you cannot tell anyone about it."

"I'm married. How can I work on a project and not tell my wife about it?"

The Colonel looked at the ceiling for a moment before facing the man. He took in a deep breath, "I can tell you this, get out of here right now."

"Wait a minute Mr. Army, I looked forward to this job's good pay."

Friday's face turned red, he pointed to the door, and yelled, "Now and I mean now."

The Colonel faced us. "Everyone take five minutes and think this over. I will ask individually if you can keep everything secret." When he stood in front of me I said, "I'm not real close to my family, we don't talk much. My passion is reading books."

The instructor gave us the rest of the day off, but we had to be near a telephone at 4:00 PM. The phone rang promptly at 4:00 and I was told to return the next day. Only four of us entered the room.

From that day forward things became a swirl. I was to be placed in a position in France where I could observe enemy military actions. Two small cameras would be used to record any and all documents that came into my possession. My orders clearly specified photographing only, no sneaking around to find facts, studying anything, or contacting people.

They would give me one or two "contacts" only known by code names. If discovered, I could freely tell the Germans the contact names, to avoid torture. These contacts could extract me if I fell under enemy suspicion. The agency issued each of us a black pill to take if we chose death over capture.

Before shipping off for England, I received a one-week pass along with another strict silence command. I took six months of salary to my parent's house. Things were bad. My father worked as a part time stage hand at a downtown theater, mother didn't work. My sister worked as a low paid employee at a mail order company.

I spent my entire bank roll on entertaining my family, buying my mother some serviceable clothes, and stocking up on food. They expressed irritation at my refusal to provide any alcohol.

I used the Chicago library as a place to take a break from them. For my going away dinner, I took them to a fancy restaurant. After explaining that I worked on a secret war project and would be gone for a long time, mother smiled, "Oh, that's nice dear, have a good trip."

The British required two months of training in data collection, German military procedures, and French social life. A submarine then 'raft landed' three of us near Caen. Partisans took us to our assignments. The underground reported that the city of Brest's German military experienced difficulty recruiting clerical help. Our government decided to send me because they wanted to observe that city's German naval activities.

The trip took three weeks because the resistance hid me at all times. I spent hours in cellars and barn lofts. During the hiding, I practiced my language skills with children and read any available newspaper, magazine, and books.

I almost froze solid when the locals, whose names I never learned, told me the only available job was a low ranking clerical position in *Gestapo Headquarters!* My training instructors made it clear that the Gestapo's responsibility concerned security and catching spies--like me. My contact, a man called Vincent, with a loud voice explained people risked their lives to get me this position. I had no choice.

Upon entering the Gestapo building I swear my body temperature dropped ten degrees and my blood turned into paste. Apparently, the sergeant directing the office understood the French populace's strong antagonism with collaborators. He was delighted to see my application, and the process remained friendly and positive. A Master Sergeant controlled all clerical operations; the only interview question he asked concerned my poor French grammar. I described my peasant background and expected my language would improve once in Brest.

I started one week later.

Assuming the Gestapo would watch me in the beginning. I spent my off-duty hours visiting the nearby library, attending operas and movies, and taking walks in various parks. On weekends I took bus rides to the shore or historical sites. Other than passing street pleasantries with neighbors and store owners, I made no friends. The Gestapo officers must have found me very boring.

My job was simple. I processed bills from French businesses for services or supplies used by the Gestapo. The forms were printed in German, but the vendors filled them out in French. After verifying that requisitions matched delivered items or services, I passed the paperwork to the sergeant who executed payment.

The headquarters building consisted of twelve stories. The sergeant repeated, on several occasions, that I and the other two French women working in the office should never go near or talk about the top four floors. Informally I learned they housed the jail, investigation, torture, and execution facilities.

In my second week I heard several distant sounding thumps. I looked at the other ladies and their faces focused on paperwork. The sergeant looked at me and with a loud voice, said, "Remember I told you not to ask any questions."

The experience was a direct dose of fear. I went to the washroom, sat on a toilet, and shook. The thump sounds occurred several times a month; each gave me another jolt of fear.

My first meeting with my contact, Vincent, occurred on opposite ends of a park bench located near the river. We had been trained to talk without moving our lips, so a casual observer would not notice any interaction between us.

I described my duties to Vincent. He would check with higher authorities to see if my work held value. If not, they would pull me out. He also fiercely warned me not to socialize with anyone because tongue slips lead to capture and unpleasant consequences.

The three of us who worked for the Gestapo faced the ostracism of the French people. So, once a week we ate dinner together. The German army held one woman's son in a prison camp and the other lived with a German soldier. The outing gave us a chance to pretend we lived normal social lives.

I created time to take document photographs by convincing the sergeant that my religion required attending a special two-hour long Friday morning novena at the cathedral.

My time would be made up by working after the office closed on Wednesday nights.

Oddly, the novena served to reinforce the slip of the tongue rule. Some of the regular attendees noticed me. They started small talking with me and after a few weeks they invited me to tea and croissant snacks after the service. I dodged the first close call when one of the ladies said, "Your French pronunciation is a little different, it sounds tinted with English."

Luckily, I fabricated an answer. "My father ran a boat supply business near Caen. He required the family to serve both the English and French boat crews. I grew up speaking both." The lady bought the story.

The slip came when one of the ladies asked about my work. I responded, "I work for a government agency that I cannot tell you about." She asked this agency's location. This question sounded innocent, so I said, "On Flower Street." The next week none of the novena attendees greeted me. The group's leader stopped me before I entered the refreshment room, and said, "Our government has no offices on Flower Street, only the German Gestapo does. Don't speak with us again."

A local book seller offered a number of classic French novels shrunk to children sized books. It matched the prayer books the novena's women carried. I spent the rest of my many dreadful novenas reading them.

For two years I took hundreds of pictures of the bills and passed them on. My contact directed me to concentrate on the hotel bills for visiting military personnel. Because my office maintained files on the various vendors, he also wanted copies of steel and concrete invoices.

The contact man added pencils to the list of bills I copied. Command decided that enlisted men used pencils, and the number ordered indicated troop movements.

The Gestapo considered only certain vacation places safe for its staff. Therefore, I spent my vacations at German resorts. The tension never left because although the staff and local people remained friendly, I never felt "Off stage." My Gestapo identification card kept away unwanted romantic advances.

For recreation I chose, as my French companions, books, the opera, walks in the park, the radio, and historical locations. But none of these helped lessen the always present fear.

We learned of the Normandy invasion when our sergeant announced the German Army would absolutely repel it. News censorship continued to sanitize reality, but rumors floated all over the market.

Then, in the late summer, things began to change.

First, the men and women who ran the upper four floors built a fire pit in the secluded parking lot. Through our office windows we saw lots of smoke.

Second, the number of high ranking visitor officers dramatically increased. They would come and stay a day or two. Their trips clearly indicated something major was happening.

Third, my landlady almost disappeared. She never wanted her peers to see her favoring the Germans. She simply rented to the market that included soldiers and civilian workers like me. She started making weekly quick visits to collect rent, but otherwise did not spend time in the building.

Fourth, the Gestapo Colonel quadrupled the pencils order. I could not believe it and carefully hid my smile while processing this requisition.

The fifth caused the most worry. The French populace began to sense the coming of freedom and expressed it with open hostility toward collaborators. Yelled insults became the norm for the walk to and from work. I never got hit by the thrown stale bread, but both of my office mates did. A rock did break one of my windows. After Germany conquered France, French police established cooperation with German police officials. Now the relationship changed, they stopped reporting people's misbehavior. The sheer number of incidents overwhelmed the German army's ability to maintain strict control.

A week after the broken window, I violated our operation rules by looking at Vincent and saying out loud, "I'm scared. These people form a mob that might drag me out. Tell your superiors to get me out, *now.*"

Two days later we met again. "Four blocks from your apartment sits Pierre's bakery. It's a safe house. When it gets too hot, walk to the place without getting noticed. Take only one change of clothes and nothing else. Be sure not to tell anyone."

The Gestapo sergeant noticed the three of us clerks becoming more nervous. He declared, "Ladies, the Gestapo will protect you; don't worry."

It didn't help. The number of shouted insults increased every day as did the number of people milling about in front of Headquarters. Neither of these things would have ever occurred if the Germans still held tight control.

Two days after the sergeant's reassurance, someone threw an empty wine bottle at me; it smashed on the wall near my head. The time to flee had arrived. A nearby store carried flamboyant prostitute's clothes; I outfitted myself. The ladies of the night begin their trade just after dark. Emulating the lady's exaggerated hip movement, I walked to Pierre's. The baker pretended to invite me in for a tryst, but quickly hid me in the basement. I took only one anthology of short stories with me and read it three times while waiting.

Three days later a man dressed as a priest came into the bakery. He gave me a nun's habit and cardboard suitcase. Together we walked to the bus stop located next to a church. The ticket took me back to the small harbor community used by the US Department, now called OSS, to take me to France.

A fishing boat captain picked me up, housed me for the night, issued men's work clothes, and, placed me in his crew for a day's work. No other OSS operative came along. The captain told me that OSS did not want the field personnel to talk to anyone.

The boat dropped me off at a small village located just east of Portsmouth. A youngish man wearing a business suit walked up and in a perfect American accent said, "Juliette, welcome home."

The words spoken in that accent acted like flipping open a pressure cooker. I started to cry and collapsed sobbing. It would take months to live without the incredible constricting band of caution, secrecy, and just plain fear.

The OSS placed me in a compound that housed eager young Americans. They were scheduled to be sent into freed Europe for the purpose of rebuilding government operations. They constantly talked about "making a difference".

When asked about my background, I said, "I worked on a secrete project and could not give any details."

We actually had nothing to talk about; I found the well-stocked compound library.

In the beginning, I tried to locate my activities within the war effort by reading old newspapers and magazines. After a short time, this activity lost it shine, and I picked up novels published while I worked in France. I guess the OSS believed that these young people could help the OSS veterans re-adjust to normal American life. For me, the opposite occurred.

Three weeks later I found myself in a London compound with ten other OSS veterans. We, during reorientation sessions with psychologists, would discuss methods to recover from the relentless pressure and fear. After two weeks of trying to learn how to reenter American life, the OSS commander held a luncheon. At it, he awarded each of us a Distinguished Service Medal, the highest military medal a civilian could earn. The metal was accompanied by strict orders not to show it to anyone nor tell how we earned it. Only the standard, "I worked on a secret project about which I can tell you nothing" could be said.

Officers received staterooms on the ship that took hundreds of enlisted men home. I shared a lower deck cubical of a stateroom with a woman lieutenant whose duty was to serve as a secretary to a general who directed a non-combat military function. To her, the war proved to be a fun adventure. We had nothing in common. I read every item in the skimpy library and ignored the ship's ruckus party atmosphere.

As we approached New York and home everyone else's excitement level rose; I did not know if any of my family still lived and doubted they even missed me. The lady I shared the stateroom with came from Chicago. From our few conversations, it sounded like the city held many more interesting opportunities than I previously experienced. The OSS offered each of us a free ticket to any city on the continent. Chicago seemed a good location for starting over. I swore not to get involved with my family's disagreeable lifestyle.

"So, what did you do when you came here," Rita asked? "The government seemed to be through with you."

"I lived off my back pay, before finding part time work. Eventually, Northwestern University's library advertised for a librarian fluent in French. After thirty years, I retired."

"Did you marry?"

I made a small laugh. "No because I never found a man who understood two important parts of me. First, I love books and they form my life's true passion. Second, and this sounds odd, but daily living in France made America's everyday trials and tribulations seem unimportant. Things like tight budgets, a disabled car, or a boyfriend breakup cannot match the intense fear of being taken upstairs for torture and death."

Looking directly at Rita, "But books are my life. I took this job to help customers find the right ones."

"Shit, after all of the crazy questions these illiterate customers ask, you should wear your medal to work every day."

I said, "Not likely."

Robert L. Nelis

Robert L Nelis began his writing career as he commuted to and from his job as a municipal official in Chicago suburbs, creating characters and laying out plots as he drove. Now retired, he enjoys having time to write the stories he planned over his twenty-seven years of commuting.

Rob received a master's degree in urban planning and policy from the University of Illinois where he also served as adjunct faculty. He lives in Chicago with his wife of 42 years in a 110-year-old house and enjoys his four grandchildren.

Miss Mimi's Charm School
By Ana Thorne

The summer of 1960, Dad signed me up for a six week class for thirteen and fourteen year old girls at Shillito's, the largest department store in downtown Cincinnati. Our family shopped at Shillito's whose elevators, escalators, and sales floors were familiar territory to me.

Dad bought his tailored suits in the men's section on the mezzanine. The previous year, after much 'weeping and gnashing of teeth' on my part, I was fitted for my first training bra in the teen department on the second floor.

Since my parent's divorce and Mother's move back to Mexico, Dad became a single father. Along with Miss Julia, a family friend, I helped take care of the household and look after my younger sister and brother.

"This flyer has all the information about the classes," Dad said as he handed me a piece of paper.

I'd never been downtown alone. I was excited at this chance to see the world without adult supervision, beyond the small, segregated society where we lived. In the city. By myself.

* * * * *

On Saturday morning, Dad helped me select a cobalt blue full skirt, matching blue and white polka-dot blouse, dress up black flats and white nylon, fold-down socks. I brushed my hair into a ponytail held in place with a rubber band.

Mother left behind a medium sized, black clutch bag in which I stored a few tissues, the flyer from Shillito's, the exact change for the round trip bus ride, and an extra dime for a phone call home in case of emergency.

* * * * *

The bus lurched forward as the quarter and the dime fell from my hand into the fare box. In my window seat, I read the flyer for the umpteenth time.

"Charm School ... Shillito's Department Store ... 7th & Race Streets ... Cincinnati Ohio ... Girls 13 and 14 ... Saturdays 10am to 12 noon ... 7th Floor."

* * * * *

The banner read 'Shillito's Charm School for Young Ladies.'

A white lady at the reception table asked, "May I help you?"

"My Dad said I'm registered," I answered.

"Are you sure you're in the right place?"

My home training didn't allow me to sass adults. A tall white woman came up to the table.

"Hello, I'm Miss Mimi," she said in a warm tone. "What is your name?"

"Inez Taylor."

She placed a polished, pink finger next to my name on the list. "Miss Barbara will give you a name tag and table assignment. Won't you Miss Barbara?"

Miss Barbara gave me a tag printed with my name, where I lived, and my table number. "Thank you, Miss Barbara," I said.

"You have nice manners, Inez," said Miss Mimi. "Go in and find your table."

Miss Mimi was stacked, statuesque, and reminded me of Mae West whom I'd seen in black and white movies on late night television. She wore a fitted dress with a narrow belt that cinched her waist and accentuated her wide hips. Matching jewelry and a diamond engagement ring completed her outfit.

Miss Mimi walked like Mae West. Her tapered dress constricted the length of the steps she took in her high heels. Small, mincing steps moved her body in a smooth, undulating motion. Miss Mimi's shapely legs were visible from just below the knee and ended in not quite slim ankles.

A fire red plastic gift bag imprinted with the Shillito's logo sat in the four chairs at table three. The bag contained small bottles of nail polish and remover, cotton balls, clippers, an emery board, cold cream, glycerin and rosewater soap and oil, a notepad and a pencil.

The tables filled with bubbly girls and Miss Mimi surveyed the room with a ruby-red lipstick smile. Her full breasts pointed straight out at us.

"Good morning, ladies. Please introduce yourselves to everyone at your table."

The three other girls traded names, their neighborhoods and schools. In a group stare, they turned to me, the only brown person in the room.

"How do you say your name?" asked Becky from Delhi Hills.

"How old are you?" asked Linda from Western Hills.

"Where is Lincoln Heights?" asked Allison from Cheviot Hills. "Are you Italian?"

200

"Eye-Nez," I answered. "Thirteen. North of the city limits. Not Italian."

The girls were unaware of the existence of the all Black town of Lincoln Heights where I lived. I didn't know the location of their neighborhoods, but I recognized the names.

I doodled on my notepad until Miss Mimi spoke again.

"Welcome to Charm School, ladies," she said. "I'm Miss Mimi and for the next five Saturdays we'll learn a lot about polish, poise, presence, polite manners, and proper etiquette."

I wrote down the 'P' words. I looked up. Becky's, Linda's and Allison's eyes gawked at me. They grinned, showed their teeth and lowered their heads.

"Ladies, remember that the trick to feeling good about yourself is to decide how you want to look, what it takes to put that look together, and how it can be accomplished with the utmost efficiency. The result should be a timeless style that suits your body shape."

I wrote 'trick, efficiency, timeless style' in my notepad.

No part of Miss Mimi's upper or lower body shook or shimmied beneath her dress. I imagined the tight dress held her like a butterfly waiting to break free of its cocoon. The contour of her legs and the voluptuousness of her 'chichis' matched her elegance. Her body reminded me of a larger form of the mannequin that stood in the corner of Mother's sewing alcove. In her accented *Ingles*, Mother might have said, "She hab on bery good girdle that cost a lot of money to her husband."

"Before we talk about skin and nail care, let's describe my outfit," Miss Mimi said. "This is important, because in the last class we'll stage a fashion show for our families and friends. Each of you will walk the runway and model an outfit of your choosing. Everything we do over the next few weeks will come together to make that moment a complete success for you."

I wrote 'fashion show.'

"Miss Mimi ran her hands down the sides of her dress. "What color is this dress?

Three girls said "pink." I said, "Peach."

"Peach is right," Miss Mimi affirmed. "What color is my belt?"

Silence. One beat. Two beats.

From a table by the window, I heard, "light beige."

I'd paid attention when Mother talked about fabrics and color and fashion styles.

"Bone," I said, showing off.

Miss Mimi looked in my direction and smiled.

We described everything Miss Mimi wore except her undergarments. Her dress was made of "silk noil, or raw silk" and her accessories were "inexpensive, but tasteful, costume jewelry."

Miss Barbara passed out bowls of warm sudsy water and hand towels as Miss Mimi inspected each girl's hands. She stopped when she looked at Allison's hands.

"I see that some of you bite your nails. You can break this bad habit by keeping your nails buffed and polished. At the end of today's lesson, your nails should look like mine."

I'd stopped biting my nails a year ago. And now, thanks to Miss Mimi, I had my first bottle of pink nail polish.

After our manicures were approved and our nail polish dried, we took a snack break. Miss Mimi stood near the cloth-covered table of cookies, punch, and triangle sandwiches without crust.

"Whenever a lady approaches food," Miss Mimi began, "she should not appear to be hungry. A little bit of food, slowly eaten and properly chewed will satisfy your appetite. It isn't good to be either underweight or overweight."

Becky asked, "How much food should we get?"

"That's a good question. Considering that you'll probably have lunch and dinner when you go home, what do you think is the polite amount to put on your plate?"

"Two sandwiches, two cookies, one punch," answered Allison.

A voice in the back asked, "Are seconds allowed?"

"Another good question," Miss Mimi said. "The answer is yes. Ideally, each of you should take two sandwiches, one cookie and a glass of punch. If you like the cookies, and after you finish your sandwiches, you may get one or two more cookies and another glass of punch. Of course, you may always take lesser amounts if you like. But a ladylike plate wouldn't be more than what I've described."

Compared to the food we ate at home, the mid-morning sugar boost was exceptionally tasteless. I'd eaten many mayonnaise sandwiches, but not with the slices of cucumbers that I slipped into my napkin. The thin cookies were sweet with a hint of lemon, but not as chewy as the oatmeal raisin cookies I liked. The watery, yellow punch didn't satisfy my thirst as much as red Kool-Aid.

Miss Mimi spent the last hour discussing exfoliation, acne, oily and dry skin, and how to protect the skin in the sun. The talk about skin discoloration confused me. Did she mean that white skin could become discolored and turn into brown skin? I didn't dare ask.

"Ladies, the jar of cold cream and the glycerin and rosewater soap and oil are for you to take home. Use the soap to wash your face and give it a warm rinse. Apply a light layer of cold cream and finish with a dab of the oil. Your skin will have a healthy glow and prep your face for the lesson on makeup. Next week will be about hair care, styles, and products. Don't forget to bring back the hand mirror from your red bag."

Miss Mimi said something to each girl as we walked out of the room.

"Allison, keep polish on those nails. Becky, watch your portions. Linda, next week we'll talk about taking care of long hair. Inez, we'll work on brightening you up."

I wasn't sure what she meant by 'brightening' me up.

* * * * *

I looked at my charm school notes on the bus ride home. On a new page, I wrote "Ask Dad" and underneath listed 'girls smiling, discoloration and brightening you up.'

Dad got the jump on me when he picked me up at the bus stop, "Did you have any trouble when you got there?"

"Miss Barbara didn't want to look for my name on the list, but the teacher, Miss Mimi, straightened it out."

"Was your name on the list?"

"Yes."

"Was it marked paid?"

"I don't know."

"How many other girls in the class?"

"I counted twenty."

"Any others like you?"

"Not a one." I told Dad what we learned, and that Miss Mimi said she was going to brighten me up. He chuckled.

"What did she mean by that?" I asked.

"Maybe Miss Mimi thinks that all you need is a bit of polish."

"I still don't get it."

"Just take it as a compliment," Dad said in the voice that I knew ended discussion on one subject, but did not necessarily close it for another.

"What is discoloration of the skin?"

"You don't have to worry about that."

"Whenever I looked up from taking notes, the three girls at my table were staring at me. And when our eyes met, they put on big grins."

Dad laughed out loud. "They stared at you because they couldn't figure out what you are. They've probably never seen anyone that looks like you before today."

"Yeah, one girl asked if I was Italian. But why do they smile?"

"They're embarrassed that they can't turn their eyes away and you caught them staring."

Just like I couldn't help staring at Miss Mimi.

"What should I say to them?"

"Don't say anything, just smile back."

*****

Mother regularly called and wrote to us, and last year she visited for a week. It had been two years since she left. I wrote a letter to tell her about the charm school classes and that I needed a dress for the fashion show. In the P.S., I wrote down my size and measurements.

Mother worked wonders with the help of a Singer sewing machine. She altered all the dresses that Dad bought for her. She removed ruffles and added lace, turned a full skirt into a straight one and added a kick pleat. To accent her cleavage, she lowered the neckline. She drew attention to her slim wrists by shortening a long-sleeved blouse to three-quarter length. She replaced buttons with zippers and brown linings in her winter coats to red or white silk. She used her creative eye to personalize and distinguish the clothes she wore and replaced the manufacturer's label with her own custom designed labels.

I wrote that I needed a fitted, knee-length, sleeveless, peach, silk dress with a round collar, and a thin belt at the waist. If Mother could copy Miss Mimi's first day outfit, I would be the hit of the fashion show.

* * * * *

At the next class, I wore my dark brown, wavy hair loose and parted on the left side. That morning, I washed my hair twice. It was clean and ready for Miss Mimi's inspection and lessons in hair care. I did not forget to bring the hand mirror.

The second week, the gift bag contained a bottle of Halo – the same shampoo that Mother used, and according to the TV ads, 'glorifies your hair.' When she left, Dad stopped buying shampoo and told us that we could use soap to wash our hair. His lack of empathy about the needs of girls made me appreciate the soft-bristled brush, comb, the tube of Alberto VO5, the can of hair spray, six pink, plastic hair rollers, and bobby pins that were also in the bag.

"Good morning, ladies. Today, I've arranged for us to visit the beauty salon in the store for a short tour. Saturday's are busy, so we'll stay just long enough to get a feel for what it takes to maintain and draw attention to your feminine assets.

* * * * *

  In the beauty salon, I remembered the story Mother told me about how Dad lost his job parking cars in the Shillito's garage. I was a babe in arms when she went to the beauty salon for a cut and curl. The ladies in the salon 'oohed and aahed' over me and made a soft pallet inside a glass enclosed display case where I slept while Mother got her hair done. Mother said that I looked like a little white baby and the ladies in the salon didn't suspect that I was the daughter of a Negro who parked cars in the garage. After her appointment, Mother went to the garage to meet Dad. The foreman saw them kiss hello and concluded that Dad was married to a white woman. That she was Mexican didn't make any difference. Mother said that Dad lost his job the next day because of the color of her skin, not his.

* * * * *

  In the salon, we saw women of all ages, shapes and sizes in various stages of renovation, restoration, repair, upgrade, improvement and general overhaul. Two Negro women worked in the salon. One swept the floor and the other provided clean towels to the ladies who shampooed hair. They surveyed our group when we came in and I smiled at them to acknowledge kinship.

  The salon operators explained each step as we watched women receive facials, haircuts, curls and color, and pedicures. Mother tweezed her eyebrows and it seemed painful, but didn't compare to the leg and moustache waxing that occurred in the salon. I watched in wonder as a strip of cloth was placed over hot wax applied directly to the skin, and then pulled off to strip away the hair at the root from the lower leg and above the top lip. I felt a little anxious because my legs were hairy and I hadn't yet started to think about shaving or waxing them.

Back in the classroom, I looked in the hand mirror and did a careful examination of my face to check for a moustache. I didn't detect any hair growth.

With Linda as a model, Miss Mimi demonstrated how to use the plastic rollers and she warned us about using too much hair spray.

"Remember, ladies, the best thing you can do for your hair is to keep it clean. You can wash it every day if you use a gentle shampoo like Halo, and if you can, use a conditioner after shampooing." I vowed to tell this tip to Dad to see if I could get a bottle of shampoo out of him.

The third week, Miss Mimi showed a slide show of fashion styles that complemented and looked best with particular female body types. We discussed cleavage, collars, waistlines, hem lines and sleeve lengths and how their proper use can help a woman show off her good points and hide her bad ones. Except for

Becky, we were a skinny group. Our problem wasn't what clothes looked best on us, but what our parents would allow us to wear.

The dress from Mother arrived after the third week of charm school. It wasn't exactly what I envisioned. It was too tight and it wasn't silk. The belt was too big and wouldn't stay closed. But I had to make it work for the fashion show.

The fourth week, our plastic bag was filled with makeup. Lipstick, eyebrow pencil, mascara, rouge, makeup compact, and eye shadow. I smiled to myself as I used the tips I'd learned from Mother when she put on her 'Elizabeth Taylor' face, as she called it.

On the fifth Saturday, the runway was set up for practice. We stood on the floor along both sides of the narrow, elevated stage while Miss Mimi gave us a lesson in how to walk.

"It's important to begin your walk on the correct foot. You must be in the ready 'T' position. Hands relaxed at your sides, left foot pointed forward, right foot behind it pointed to the right."

Miss Mimi took the 'T' stand and walked down the runway, one foot in front of the other, as she talked us through the process. My eyes followed Miss Mimi's legs up the runway. Her calf muscles flexed in her heels when she lifted her foot to take the next step. At the end of the runway, she stood like a statue.

Everyone strained to see the top of the stage and how Miss Mimi's feet were positioned.

"Stand firm in this position for two to three seconds. No longer. The next cue will be your signal to pivot. Watch carefully."

Miss Mimi balanced her body on the balls of her feet and slowly twirled around to face the back of the stage. Once again, she was in the 'T' position, poised to walk back up the runway. Even in that twirling move, Miss Mimi's body stayed solid and stable. As she took her first step back, I heard a swishing sound. Like undergarments and nylons coming in close contact with one another.

As part of our introduction at the fashion show, Miss Mimi would read where we lived and the name of the high school that we would attend in September. I submitted the name of the high school I'd chosen, but I wasn't sure if Dad could afford the tuition. I wondered if charm school cost more than real school.

* * * * *

Dad, his friend, Julia, and my sister and brother attended the fashion show and reception. I wore the small amount of makeup that Dad allowed. I'd slept in rollers all night and combed out the tight curls into a soft, symmetrical style. Miss Mimi was at the microphone. My turn down the runway.

"Ladies and gentlemen, Miss Inez Taylor lives in Lincoln Heights and will enter the ninth grade at Mount Notre Dame High School for Girls in the fall."

On "ladies" I came through the stage curtain with a big smile on my face and took the top of the runway 'T' position.

On "Girls" I started the walk down the runway, one foot in front of the other. I held on tight to Mother's bag.

"Today, Inez is wearing a hot pink, cotton-brocade, sleeveless, summer dress."

If I didn't slow down, I'd be forced to pivot sooner than I'd rehearsed.

"The fitted dress zips up the back and cinches at the waist with a wide belt that wraps through a white buckle in the front."

I reached the pivot point way ahead of cue.

"Inez' outfit is highlighted by a pair of black, patent-leather spoolie pumps and matching clutch purse."

I stood there for a moment in the perfect "T" position, pointed my toe to draw attention to my shoes and brought the purse up toward my face to give the audience a better look.

"Her tasteful gold hoop earrings and matching bracelets …"

I slanted my neck to the right and to the left to show off the earrings, and bent my arm at the elbow to show the bracelets.

"… brighten and finish her pink, black and white accented ensemble."

On "brighten" I pivoted and walked back up the runway.

"Doesn't she look lovely?"

I heard the same polite applause the audience had given to each girl before me.

"Thank you, Inez."

I reached the curtain and turned to face the audience one last time, and then exited stage left as the next girl was introduced.

At the grand finale, all the girls were on stage. Miss Mimi introduced us again and awarded us with a certificate of completion. The Shillito's photographer took a group photo.

Everyone was happy and smiling, including me.

Julia sat with my sister and brother while they ate the same refreshments served in our first class. I took Dad to sign the guest book. Miss Mimi stood nearby with her back to him and somehow they bumped into each other.

"Excuse me," Dad said.

"No harm done," Miss Mimi replied. "Are you with Inez?"

"I'm her father."

"Oh, I see. Well, she's a very smart young lady and pretty too. She did well in the class and on the runway. You should be proud of her."

Dad put his arm around me. "She's a pretty good kid. We're thinking about keeping her."

They both laughed at the joke I'd heard a million times. Miss Mimi started to move away from the table and Dad followed her. I went for cookies, but my eyes followed Miss Mimi. She stopped to face Dad. He had a big smile on his face that showed all his teeth. He leaned into her body space, put his left hand on her right elbow and steered her toward the space where the runway met the wall. He whispered something to Miss Mimi and her head gave a slight jerk. She looked in my direction and our eyes met. She moved away from the wall to keep from being cornered by Dad.

"I wanted to thank you for taking such an interest in my daughter. These classes have done wonders for her."

"I was just doing my job. Excuse me, please."

Miss Mimi walked to the other side of the room and began talking with a group of white men wearing gray suits. Dad's jaw shortened and his wolfish grin disappeared into his closed mouth. He picked up a glass of yellow punch.

finis

Ana Thorne

Ana lives with her granddaughter in the Carolinas by way of Los Angeles, the Virgin Islands, New York City, Oakland, San Francisco, Seattle and Cincinnati. With an MFA in Creative Writing and a doctorate in Cultural Studies, Ana teaches nonfiction writing classes, film studies, English, and Africana studies online and in the classroom. Her short story, *No Thank You, Otto Titzling*, appeared in the *Santa Fe Online Journal* and the *Two Hawks Quarterly*. She is a reviewer at large for the Association of Graduate Liberal Studies Program publications, *Confluence* and *Western Tributaries*. In homage to her Dad, a former Negro League baseball player, she maintains a visual research/digital storytelling website, www.thomasturnernegroleague.org. Ana writes stories about her experiences growing up as an African American/Mexican (Blaxicana) baby boomer in the Midwest and is currently working with the 2018 cohort of the Charlotte Lit's Author's Lab to complete a memoir.

1200 Rupees
By Nancy Zupanec

We gathered at a dirty, noisy office to begin our journey to the end of the earth. The office wasn't easy to spot. Lanes spread out and around it like lava flows. Most of the buildings in the area were tucked into hiding places, waiting to be found. The many people milling in front of the office helped shield its location, although people milled in front of everything in India. Miniscule and plain, the sign that announced the name of the business only made the office easier to miss, and I walked right past it twice.

I didn't understand what to expect on the journey. I thought I did. I thought I was buying a ticket for a trek into the desert on the back of a camel. I'd read the flyers. Like most sales pitches, the brochures had no doubt exaggerated, promising a magical experience with guides and camels and desert and a glorious sunset. The trip would be more magical, the flyers had read, by extending the visit with a night spent in a tent on the sand. Even accounting for puffery, the trip sounded thrilling. 1200 rupees. $17.80. There was no haggling. The price felt fair especially in hindsight when I realized that for 1200 rupees, I'd purchased eternity and immortality. Not for me, mind you, but the cost of the trek had included glimpses of both.

I wasn't alone on the trip. We were four Americans and one Netherlander, all heading off for an afternoon and evening in the unknown. Although I felt eager for the adventure, I wouldn't have traveled halfway around the world to journey into the Indian desert. It so happened that I was in the neighborhood and saw the opportunity as the once-in-a-lifetime kind. The camels, symbols of the exotic, intrigued me more than anything. I didn't think I'd be afraid of them, plus I'd learned somewhere along the way to beware of a camel's inclination to spit.

We trekkers left the dirty office and followed our driver to a parking lot a short distance away. None of us said much. There were just a few murmurs as we made our way across the pavement. The driver gestured toward a vehicle and we assumed we were to climb aboard. Our 1200 rupees trip was to begin with a ride in an ancient jeep. The jeep's dents and dust signaled it had made the journey many times.

We were not so much crowded as we were jammed onto benches in the back of the jeep. Our legs crossed and uncrossed whenever they could find a tiny opening, although we tried to prevent them from brushing against any leg not our own. I don't know about the Netherlander, but we Americans are well versed in the psychological necessity of honoring each other's personal space.

Since we couldn't move, we settled in and tried to figure out something to do. One American, the self-designated leader, started a random conversation with another trekker squeezed in on the opposite bench.

"Hey, my name is James," he said. "My friend Sara and I are visiting from Wisconsin. We're in grad school in Madison. What about you?"

I was relieved he'd broken the ice because I knew we couldn't just sit and stare at each other. We didn't have any windows as an alternative to conversation. Canvas blew in their place. If we'd wanted the diversion of exploring our surroundings visually, our only option would have been to gaze out the back of the jeep, but holding our heads sideways would have strained our necks and offered a dusty view of the past at best.

We began our journey on something resembling a road. Even though it was paved, the road had deteriorated into potholes. The driver didn't have much room to navigate around them so he drove straight through. At particularly lurching moments I worried that the experience we were having might be the promised adventure. If my mind began to wander, perhaps to the vision of a cool, quiet café, the road jolted me back to reality.

After a short time I discovered that the potholed road was princely compared to what was to come. The pavement morphed into pebbles. The brochure hadn't said anything about pebble roads. Where were the camels? Where was the desert?

After the pavement and the pebbles came nothing, just the land itself, providing the roughest ride of all. No pretense of a road—just the earth with small brown shrubs laying claim to tiny patches of dirt, and rocks interrupting the landscape unpredictably. I thought about the fact we'd have to return the same way we'd come.

I was grateful for the presence of the other squeezed passengers. We could band together if the jeep broke down or if the jeep driver turned out to be a kidnapper who planned to take us to the middle of nowhere and hold us for ransom. While the latter scenario verged on improbable, the former didn't. My life was in the hands of a man I'd met thirty minutes earlier and a jeep last serviced ten years before at best. While most trekkers hadn't been able to leave their phones behind, it was hard to believe they'd find cell service in such remoteness. Here I would be—the hero of a disaster I'd inflicted on myself—starved to death in a place where no one would think to look for my body.

Eventually our cramming on the benches led to slowed circulation in arms and legs, and then to numbness. When the jeep came to a rumbling halt, the driver—who was also our guide—asked us to climb out. His English was patchy but we got the idea and required very little coaxing to edge off the benches and step onto the ground.

Standing was hard and walking even more difficult, although I attributed our problems less to the cramping and more to the wind that was blowing crazily. I'd noticed the billowing of the canvas windows along the way, but the hurricane winds in this place took me by surprise.

We received an unexpected gift when one of the Americans turned out to be fluent in Hindi, the language spoken in this part of India. She became our interpreter, our lifeline. The guide had attempted to explain the unusual presence of wind but we didn't understand.

After he offered the explanation directly to our interpreter, she was able to untangle the guide's comments for us, although we would have chosen the ability to remain upright over the explanation of why standing was so hard. Reasons wouldn't hold our feet steady. Meanwhile we saw no camels, just the disarray the wind was stirring up.

I looked hard at the parched surroundings. I saw trees in the arid landscape. I saw a small structure I assumed was a house. I saw a second small structure that turned out to be a shrine. Since I was a newcomer to India, I didn't know that Hindu and Muslim shrines popped up everywhere, even in remote locations. Somehow I didn't think we'd come to see the house or the shrine, though, and I was right. The guide told us via our interpreter that the smudged, dusty area we'd reached was an oasis. I had to question the interpreter's knowledge of the language because nothing green or fertile was in sight. I also considered the possibility that in Hindi, oasis doesn't really mean oasis.

I saw a small, shallow pond dotted with a few short trees bearing foliage that was a dirty gray. Most of the trees leaned permanently to one side, which raised questions about how abnormal the winds were. I had to call the concave area in front of my eyes a pond because it contained water, but water so brown it was barely distinguishable from the caramel-colored earth surrounding it.

We didn't stay long. Just long enough to marvel at what passed for an oasis and to take pictures of it with our sandy camera lenses. Although the idea of being jammed back into the jeep wasn't pleasing, neither was the idea of standing near the pond until we became grit figures unrecognizable to our own mothers.

It was in this remoteness that I began to feel something powerful. It was a sprouting sense of pride. While the dented jeep said that others had ventured on this trek before and the noisy office had made clear that others would venture on it again, I felt special. I wasn't the only person who'd seen or would see the bent trees and murky water, but I could pretend I was. To me the area felt distinctive and rare. Uncharted and ancient. The end of the earth. I decided the bumpy, brown landscape represented a world as tucked away as the office we'd departed from, and I'd found them both.

The cramped jeep ride seemed to have no end. Since we weren't traveling on a road, I can only say that somewhere after our oasis stop, the jeep turned, jolted over several rocks, and headed off in a different direction. When the jeep finally staggered to a stop, brakes scrunching, there they were—seven camels. Five for the desert-seekers, one for the guide, and one for another man who'd been overseeing the animals. He shared the camel with his young son who'd accompanied him.

"Would you look at that?" said the Netherlander. "Those camels are huge. I think I'm nervous."

"No worries," replied James. "I'll bet the camels are pretty tame. Plus we have the guide to keep everything neat and tidy."

Sara nodded.

I don't know whether it's more accurate to say that the camels were sitting on the ground or lying down, but they were definitely not standing up. As we drew closer to them, still on our benches in the jeep, we could see brilliant, multi-colored spreads on the camels' backs, as well as boxes of supplies tied to the spreads. The camels had bands of cloth woven into rings that rested on top of their heads like halos. Although I'd seen camels in zoos and photographs, I was about to sit on one of the multi-colored spreads with a camel underneath and ride away. Just 1200 rupees.

My menacing thoughts about the jeep driver resurfaced for a moment. We were now that much farther away from our starting point, and I wasn't convinced that anyone looking for our bodies would choose to endure the semi-road, the pebbles, the shrubs, and the rocks to search for us. Our skeletons would lie in the arid terrain, dried like buffalo bones in the Plains.

After our rugged journey to what was really the starting point of the trek, I imagined the guide would give us pause to take in our surroundings. I thought we'd be able to wander among the camels, reflecting on their size and appearance and what it felt like to be in their midst. It was a breath-taking moment, but one that ended as quickly as it had begun.

The jeep driver gestured for us to choose an animal and sit down. I wasn't sure how to go about selecting one other than to place myself on the back of the only camel remaining riderless. On top of the spreads were saddle-like objects with horns to grasp, and I gripped mine tightly. Everyone was giddy. The camel ride was about to start.

I didn't know anything about how to ride on a camel, although I'd been on an elephant in an Indian national park once. As the elephant had crashed through tall growth that had masqueraded as a path, as it had grabbed leaves with its outstretched trunk, I'd visualized myself losing my balance and tumbling down hard. But even with time spent riding on an elephant, I felt inexperienced in the art of sitting on the back of a huge animal that could pitch me to the ground and stomp on me if the mood struck.

The jeep driver walked past each of us. "Time to go."

He indicated we needed to start, which meant the camels had to stand. As I wondered how they would do that, the jeep driver approached me. He said something about leaning back but before I got a chance to digest his words and consider when and how far to lean, the camel arose, first two legs and then the other two. Although everything seemed to happen in a split second, it still left plenty of time to hang on or fall. It occurred to me that riding a camel might be like flying on a plane, with take-off and landing the hard parts.

I gazed around in amazement. I was on the back of a camel. I gripped hard on the horn as though my life depended on it, which might have been true given the fierce, abnormal winds that continued to spin around and around.

The jeep driver made a sort of clicking noise to the camels that meant, "Get going." The camels were lined up one after another with a rope attached to each so that they would step in sync. The sight reminded me of children in preschool who walked holding onto a rope so the teacher wouldn't lose any of them. I imagined that our camels weren't placed in line randomly. Maybe one of them was fond of kicking the others whenever it could. This camel was probably positioned right in front of the jeep driver who could tell the camel to behave with a different clicking sound.

The Netherlander and her camel went first, I was second, the Hindi speaker third, the other two Americans, and finally the jeep driver and the camel-minder. The camel-minder's young son walked alongside the lead camel holding onto her reins. But after we'd traveled a short distance, the boy tossed the reins upward for the Netherlander to grab and headed toward the back of the line. How could he do that? Even though he was a child, he'd been tasked with leading us. He couldn't just quit and walk away.

I was unnerved by the fact that the boy had placed a complete novice in control. I guessed she was holding her breath and waiting for the boy's return, but he didn't come back and we plodded on just the same.

Slowly I came to understand that no one on the ground had to hold the camel's reins in order to direct the journey. The guide had placed the lead camel in front for a reason. This camel knew exactly where to turn and where to continue straight. Past shrubs, up inclines, and around large rocks. There was no reason to be concerned. Our guide was wise and impeccably trained. There was just a flutter of friskiness as the camel lunged for an occasional leaf on an occasional shrub. I could hear a clicking noise from the back, and the camel turned its head and walked on.

The camel behind mine sneaked as far out of line as she could, tiny bells jingling from the halo on her head. My camel ignored the goings-on in front and behind. He was more interested in spitting. I'd been warned, but no one's advice had taken gale force winds into account. My camel lifted his head three or four times and let loose the spit that would typically fall to the ground but was instead driven back toward me by the relentless gusts.

I don't know how long we walked. I didn't have a watch and wouldn't have looked at it if I did. The farther we traveled into the desert and the longer we rode in near silence, the calmer I began to feel. As I crossed through the arid landscape, I could almost believe that nothing existed except this place. I found it hard to call up my personal anxieties and while external events—earthquakes, military coups, plunging stock markets—

might occur, they would happen in areas so remote from me as to be nonexistent. Just as a language that doesn't have words for numbers or colors, so the language of the desert has no names for these crises.

In this place I sensed life stripped to its essentials, which sounds contrived but offers a true picture of the sand and the brush and the rocks and the sky and the wind. These were what mattered. They'd existed in this place long before I'd arrived in the world and would continue into a future that wouldn't include me.

From on top of my camel I journeyed through the uncharted and ancient. I wasn't contained by boundaries. I saw nothing in any direction that forced me into a measurement of distance or an identification of location. No important variations in landscape, no signs noting where one city started or another ended.

Time was absent, too. There were no schedules or appointments. Of course, the sun rose and set, the rains came and went, all of which might have been offered to prove the passage of time, except for the impossibility of measuring the minutes of the uncharted and ancient. My reflections came to rest on a single thought. I was in the calmest, quietest, safest place in the world, this ground on which my camel and I walked.

As the trek continued, I began to see rolling hills of sand in the distance. They looked like the dunes in desert movies but so far away that I couldn't imagine our trek lasting long enough for us to reach them. I had faith in our camel guide, though. She would direct us to the place we were supposed to go. It would either be the dunes I could view in the distance or it wouldn't.

Since our pace didn't increase, the sand dunes must have appeared farther away than they were. We drew closer and closer until the mountains of sand lay right in front of us. I was now as eager to dismount my camel as I'd been to get on. Naturally I faced the reverse of the process that had confounded me on the front end, my new dilemma involving how camels go from standing to sitting or lying down. The jeep driver didn't provide even minimal instruction and as I continued to grip the horn, my camel hit the ground with a heavy plunk. Springing from the multi-colored spread, I tore off my shoes and socks. The wind in this place blasted more ferociously than anywhere we'd been on the trek thus far. Taking my first steps I fell, but neither the blasts of air nor the squirreliness of the sand would keep me from my adventure.

Before me rose the dunes, grains upon infinite grains of sand, filling the space with mustard-colored mountains that stretched up toward a limitless sky and out to an unreachable horizon.

We trekkers found our own paths through this slice of desert, each of us seeking the something that had driven us to the dirty, noisy office in the first place. As I swayed on top of my personal dune, the ruler of my bit of the universe, I glanced down at my feet—willing them to hold me upright. My field of vision narrowed to include the sight of a black beetle crawling across the sand. It astonished me with its aloneness, an isolation that equaled the vastness of its surroundings. In the scale of this setting, the beetle's presence on the sand took up less space than the size of a pinprick, no more room than a tiny period buried at the end of an eternal sentence.

I couldn't know a thing about the beetle's journey. I couldn't know where it had come from or where it was going or whether it would live until it got there. But for a few seconds I could look at the unlikely couple--beetle and desert--as they dazzled below me in black and gold.

I talked about the 1200 rupees price tag that bought not only a camel trek but also a glimpse of the eternal and immortal, and this is where I found them. In the dunes and the brush, in the wind and the sunset and the rocks. Not a specific dune because the sands shifted, nor a specific sunset because each one differed. Collectively, though, both eternity and immortality lived in this desert.

I dismissed all ideas of past and future trekkers coming to this place, and I claimed possession of the eternal and immortal, the ancient and uncharted, for myself.

As the afternoon wore on, the five of us found each other again and collapsed on the dunes to witness the symbol of the day's end. The setting sun didn't hurry its descent. The sun fell bit by dimming bit to the horizon and into the dunes and was gone.

We didn't ride the camels back to the place where we'd mounted. The trip would have taken too long so while we were busy in the dunes, the camel-minder had herded the camels home. The now familiar dented, dusty jeep had reappeared to pick us up. There would be no camels, no spit, no bells, no clicking sounds, only a car ride in the dark.

We took a different route home but we still bumped over rocks, pebbles, and potholes until we eventually creaked to a stop in the parking lot where we'd climbed into the jeep hours before. I thanked the driver for everything, adding the smile that I believed to be a universal symbol of appreciation.

I hadn't expected to make life-long friends on this trip. I had just wanted to be with a group of people who didn't argue a lot or speak too loudly, and that's what I got. Still, my grateful good-bye to my fellow travelers included a wistful farewell to the 1200 rupees trek.

As the others strolled off in various directions, I continued to stand next to the now empty jeep. I wanted a chance to secure, to tie down and anchor, the calm, the quiet, and the safety I'd found in the desert. They were the foundations of the freshest new memories I'd formed.

I rewound and replayed my experience. Guides, camels, desert, sunset. Eternity and immortality. I remained in the presence of all these as I lingered in the parking lot, and even as I stood effortlessly still, I could feel the fierce, abnormal wind continue to blast grains of sand into the night.

Nancy Zupanec

Nancy Zupanec was born and raised in western Massachusetts and considers herself a New Englander no matter where she lives. After closing shop on her legal career a couple of years ago, she found herself free to write pieces that weren't required to be logical. That's one reason she loves the "creative" in creative nonfiction. Her greatest accomplishment thus far is the memoir she has completed. She knows she won't be able to declare victory until the revisions are done, but she believes herself up to the task.

Nancy is fond of traveling and gets ideas for pieces through her adventures, such as the trip to India that produced "1200 Rupees." Next she plans to move on to Slovenian stories gleaned from time spent in her grandparents' homeland. She doesn't believe that distant travel is necessary to see or learn new things, though. She can just sit still and pay attention.

Living Springs Publishers

We hope you enjoyed this book. Please let us know what you think about it. You can leave a review on the book page of our website.

All of our *Stories Through The Ages* books can be found at www.LivingSpringsPublishers.com as well as on Amazon.

In 2019 we will expand our College Edition contest by allowing entries from any adult born 1965 and later. We will call this contest *Stories Through The Ages Generations Plus.* We will continue to have the Baby Boomers Plus contest for people born 1964 and earlier.

We also offer a service to help people publish a Legacy book. This could be their memoirs, combination of memories and pictures, or just about anything people want it to be.

Visit us on our website and Facebook and learn more about our contests and books.